Books in the Hard Knocks High Series

Project Windows

Darkskin and Redbones

Chapter 1

ignorant girls who tease you, know not what they speak/
the jokes on them, 'cause ya melanin is on fleek/

"*You so black! You so black! You so black!*" repeated over and over in Mahogany Brown's mind like the chorus to a sad song, killing her soul softly. The repetitive chant echoing in Mahogany's head was similar to the old soul records Dad used to play on the ancient record player every Saturday night in the living room of their apartment. The dusty black vinyl had deep scratches in the grooves and would always skip and repeat a three-second melody over and over...*Makes me wanna holla...Scratch!...Makes me wanna holla...Scratch!* When Mahogany could no longer stand the soulful crooning of Marvin Gaye, she would drown out the "old people's music" by cranking up the tunes on her iPhone or by sealing her bedroom door shut. Unfortunately for Mahogany, who was standing just outside of the pizza shop, her headphones were tucked away in her nightstand drawer, and there weren't any doors in her mind that would allow her to seal off the tormenting lyrics.

"*You so black...You so black...You so black...*" continued to perform on the center stage of her brain. Way in the back of her head, somewhere behind the curtains of her mind, an anxious voice that sounded like Mahogany's voice in the shower sang in a whisper, "*I know I look good...I know I look good...I know I look good.*" She recognized her own voice, but it was difficult to hear it when the chorus in the front of her mind was getting louder by the second: "*You so black! You so black! You so black*!" The conductor of the chorus was stuck-up, Malikah Shabazz. She was the one that cracked the "*you so black*" joke about Mahogany that turned the entire pizza shop into a comedy club as patrons were falling out of their chairs with laughter.

If it wasn't for Vaughn Little, there's a good chance Mahogany would still be in the pizza shop, ripping all of Malikah's good hair from her scalp and raking her nails across the girl's caramel face. The laughter, the finger pointing, and the taunting from her peers infuriated Mahogany, causing her to shove Malikah against one of the tables. After the owner ran from behind the counter and intervened, Vaughn grabbed Mahogany by her arm just before both girls got tangled up and ushered her through the entrance of the pizza shop.

"Don't trip, Mahogany," Vaughn said, standing between Mahogany and the door. "She ain't *all that* anyway."

"Oh, yeah? Then why did Tafari dump me for her?" Mahogany snapped, glaring through the pizza shop glass at Malikah and Tafari sitting across from each other in a booth.

"That's because Tafari is too stupid to recognize what a great thing he had with you." Vaughn grinned. "I know if I was him, I would never pick another girl over you." The comment comforted Mahogany, briefly, like a quick hug from a friend. That was all Mahogany viewed Vaughn as, *a friend*. But Vaughn's comment suggested that he wanted more.

She had known Vaughn for years. They had most of the same classes at Bronx High, and by no coincidence he usually found a seat right beside Mahogany. English, art, orchestra—it didn't matter the class; every time Mahogany looked up from her desk or from behind her viola, Vaughn was sitting right beside her, staring and grinning that same toothy grin.

Mahogany enjoyed the attention Vaughn's eyes gave to her because there weren't many *eyes* that did. But she hated the fact that his eyes were beneath hers. Vaughn was short. And Mahogany wasn't tall by any means. In fact, she always thought of herself as being short for a girl. But the fact that she could count the dandruff flakes on top of Vaughn's peanut head bothered the heck out of her. That was the main reason why she never really considered him. Not the dandruff, but his lack of height.

"I appreciate the compliment, Vaughn," Mahogany said. "But it's obvious why Tafari chose Malikah over me."

"Why?"

"Look at me," Mahogany requested, spreading her arms like wings. "I'm dark-skinned, and my hair is kinky and not very long. How can I compete with someone like Malikah? She's light-skinned with long, flowing hair. That's what all guys want anyway, right?"

"Light-skinned girls like Malikah are trophies for insecure guys like Tafari that don't love themselves," Vaughn explained. "Plus, it's not about what's on the outside, but what's on the inside that counts."

"Thanks for calling me ugly, Vaughn."

"When did I call you ugly?" Vaughn asked, confusion wrinkling his face.

"Whenever someone says to a person, 'it's what's on the inside that counts,' they are pretty much telling that person that they are ugly on the outside."

"You know that's not what I meant—"

"Either way, I agree with you," Mahogany said, pausing to peek at her reflection in the pizza shop glass window. "This might sound strange, but I hate my face so much that I can't keep from staring at it. For hours, I stare *at* my face, *in* my face, and *through* my face, searching for something to love about it; a beauty mark, *something*. But I could never find it. Until one day I saw it in Tafari's eyes. It was like he found something in my face that I had been searching for *for* years. Tafari looked at me like no other boy ever did. He looked at me like those boys on the corner be looking at them light-skinned girls that walk by. Over those last couple of weeks while I was going out with Tafari, he made me feel like *I* was light-skinned. I felt like I was beautiful. Until today, when I saw him in the pizza shop with Malikah. That's when reality set in, and now I'm back to being the same ole, black and…" Sobs interrupted the rest of Mahogany's sentence.

"Just because you're brown-skinned doesn't mean you're not beautiful," Vaughn reasoned. "Beauty comes in all colors. Don't let social media and magazine covers dictate what's beautiful and what's not. Mahogany, you are the most beautiful girl I know."

Mahogany smirked at Vaughn while dabbing moisture from her eyes with her fingertips. Mahogany glared at Tafari and Malikah one last time before throwing her hands in the air. "I gotta get outta here."

"Lemme walk you to your building?" Vaughn requested.

"Maybe next time," Mahogany said, shaking her head. "I need to be alone so I can think."

"Are you sure?"

"Yes, I'm sure. But thanks anyway."

"So, um…I guess I'll see you in school tomorrow."

"Yeah, I'll see you tomorrow."

"Later, Mahogany."

"Bye, Vaughn." Vaughn leaned toward Mahogany for a hug, but Mahogany's body shrunk away, so he pulled back immediately. With disappointment in his face, Vaughn waved at Mahogany, turned, and walked up the block.

Mahogany gave herself her usual pep talk before stepping out into the world: *"Alright, Mahogany, keep ya chin up, eyes open, ya shoulders back, and put one foot in front of the other."* She swallowed a mouthful of air before strutting down the busy sidewalk like a hood-model. Each concentrated step suggested confidence, but her calm outward appearance was a contradiction to the thunderous storm of doubt and grief brewing on the inside. As Mahogany strode up the block, she approached two teenage boys hanging out on the corner, leaning against a light pole. Mahogany smirked when she noticed the boys gawking at her. Not at her face, though. At her body.

During the summer between ninth and tenth grade, Mahogany's body swelled in all the right places. Her mom swore up and down that her summer diet of Chicken McNuggets was responsible; she claimed they pumped up the chickens with all kinds of hormones.

Mahogany's looks rarely attracted *looks* from onlookers, so she wasn't really sure how to act or what to do. She arched her eyebrows and opened her eyes wide because the anxious voice inside told her that her eyes were her best feature. Mahogany peered straight ahead as she placed one foot in front of the other, slightly swaying her hips from side to side, shaking what the McNuggets gave her. *Chin up, shoulders back; move them hips and don't make eye contact.*

"She got a bangin' body, yo," one of the boys mentioned, loud enough for Mahogany to hear. Slowly, a smile etched across Mahogany's lips as she turned toward the corner thugs; ready to accept more complimentary words. The brown-skinned, ashy-faced dude removed the hood from his bald head and squinted as if examining Mahogany's face. "But I don't like dark-skinned girls."

"Yeah, me neither. I be likin' dem redbones." Their comments were like bricks, slapping Mahogany upside her head. The weight of the comments made her shoulders slouch and knocked the sway out of her hips. Mahogany's outer self now mirrored the constant hurricane of uncertainty that was stirring within as she dragged herself and the weighty comments toward her building.

Not only did Mahogany carry Malikah's comments with her to school the next day, but the added weight of the remarks from the corner boys made her sluggish, like the crazy lady who be carrying all those bags while she shuffles across the big park on the Southside, feeding pigeons. Mahogany took a seat in art class and put her head down on the desk. On the front stage of her brain, chants of "*you so black*" mixed superbly with the chorus of "*I don't like dark-skinned girls*," like a DJ scratching two records back and forth on two turntables. Mahogany's nerves were breakdancing inside, and her churning stomach was doing windmills. The head noise made her "*wanna holla*!"

Mahogany felt a poke on her right shoulder. Slowly, she lifted her head, and through a hazy view she saw Vaughn taking a seat beside her. "What's the matter?" Vaughn asked, concern in his voice. "You look sad. Is everything okay?"

"I'm fine," Mahogany assured.

"You ain't still trippin' off what Malikah said yesterday, are you?"

"No...no, of course not," Mahogany said, unconvincingly. Vaughn's response was interrupted by laughter coming from the back of the class. Mahogany turned in her seat and spotted Nevaeh and Nyla, whispering, laughing, and pointing at her. Mahogany couldn't quite make out what they were saying, but whatever was being said caused the students sitting near them to burst out laughing.

"Alright class, settle down!" Mrs. Mourningway called out from the front of the classroom. "The learning objective this week is perspective drawing and foreshortening. Who remembers the definition of perspective and foreshortening?"

"I do!" Zuri called out, who sat a few seats to the left of Mahogany. "When we see an object in a drawing or painting from perspective, we are seeing it from an angle that causes the part that is closest to us to appear larger than the one that is farther away. When the object is getting smaller or shorter, it is being foreshortened."

"Excellent job, Zuri," Mrs. Mourningway praised. A few girls in the back sucked their teeth at Mrs. Mourningway's words of appraisal toward Zuri. "Okay class, take out the sketches of the cylinders and blocks that we were working on yesterday. As you are working, refer to the perspective drawing examples displayed in the front of the room."

Just as the class began drawing, Mahogany took another backward glance at Nevaeh and Nyla. She noticed a crinkled piece of paper being passed from Nevaeh to Nyla and then to the boy beside her. She watched as each student scanned the paper, then burst out laughing before passing the loose leaf to the next awaiting hand. The only student in class who refused to partake in the note-passing was Noni. She sat in front of the class in a seat closest to the window. The boy who sat directly behind Noni tapped her on the shoulder and extended the paper toward her. Noni removed her ear plugs and hoody, revealing her long box braids that resembled thin black ropes. She glared at the boy for a few seconds before putting her ear plugs back in, her hoody back on, and her head back down. The boy reached around Noni and passed it to the student beside her. Mahogany's eyes followed the paper around the classroom, passing from hand to hand, until it eventually made its way to Vaughn. He was the first one to come across the crinkled loose leaf who didn't follow it up with a laugh. In fact, the more he stared, the more agitated his face grew. Vaughn grimaced, frowned, looked away in disgust, and pounded his fist on the desk. He popped out of his seat and turned toward the back of the class. "Yo, this is messed up!"

"Vaughn! Have a seat!" Mrs. Mourningway insisted as she knelt beside Zuri, helping her with her sketch. Vaughn plopped down in his chair but continued to turn in his seat and frown at Nevaeh and Nyla.

"What's the matter, Vaughn?" Mahogany asked. Vaughn glanced at Mahogany and shook his head.

"Let me see," Mahogany said, reaching for the paper.

"You don't need to see this." Vaughn moved the paper just out of her reach before turning toward the back of the class again. While Vaughn was mean-mugging Nevaeh and Nyla, Mahogany snuck the paper from his desk. Her breath was snatched from her mouth when she held the paper before her eyes. It was a sketch of a girl whose face was colored in with a black permanent marker. Her hair reached just above her shoulders, and she had an overexaggerated nose spread across her face.

There were words at the bottom of the page, but her eyes were too watery to make them out. Mahogany cleared the mist away with the back of her hand, but just as quickly, her vision was blurry again, similar to a car windshield during a rain storm. Her hands were working like windshield wipers, back and forth across her eyes, leaving just seconds to scan the words below the sketch. In capital letters, it read: SOY SAUCE. She turned off the wipers. Tears completely blinded Mahogany's vision. She lost complete control of herself, and her feelings crashed and shattered inside. Mahogany's fingers went limp, and the paper slipped to the desk. Her cupped hands held her face inches away from her wooden desk.

"Yo, forget them," Vaughn said, leaning over and placing his hand on Mahogany's shoulder. "They ain't got nothin' on you. They jealous." Through quiet sobs, Mahogany heard snickering coming from the back of the classroom. She didn't need to turn around to know that it was Nevaeh and Nyla laughing at her. In fact, it felt like half the class was laughing at her. Mahogany looked over the wreck of herself and felt overwhelmed by the crushing weight of sadness.

"May I go to the restroom, please," Mahogany asked, raising her hand in the air.

"Yes, just make sure you sign out," Mrs. Mourningway answered. "Before you go, I have some good news to share with you." Mrs. Mourningway met Mahogany at the door just before she left the classroom. "I was going to tell you at the end of class, but I might as well tell you now. I entered one of your drawings into the tapestry exhibit for youth art month coming up in the spring," she said, beaming.

"Thank you, Mrs. Mourningway," Mahogany said, barely above a whisper.

"Thank you? That's it! Where's the excitement?"

"I am excited. It's just that, um—"

"Do you know that I have a total of one hundred and thirty students in all of my art classes? And out of those one hundred and thirty students, I felt that only you and three other students had paintings that were worthy enough to be displayed in the art exhibit. Your artwork will be displayed amongst the best youth artists from high schools all across New York City. You should be ecstatic!"

"I am…it's just that—" Mahogany paused to swallow the lump forming in her throat. She glanced at Nevaeh and Nyla, who were still laughing and pointing at her, and decided she couldn't take it anymore. "I gotta go, Mrs. Mourningway." Mahogany hurried into the girls' restroom, locked herself in one of the stalls, and wept into her open palms until she was all cried out. Slowly, anger seeped into Mahogany's body, as if it were entering through her pores, starting at her fingers. A shade of crimson red replaced the mist in her eyes, but still, she could barely see. Pictures of Nevaeh and Nyla's smug faces developed in the darkroom of her mind and flashed before her eyes. Her fingers balled into tight fists and fired from her side, punching through images of Nevaeh and Nyla's faces and slamming into the metal stall door. Grunts and yelps escaped through her tightly pursed lips with each blow. Thirty seconds later, she fell into a seated position on top of the toilet after the anger had been completely drained from her body through her fists. Mahogany examined her knuckles, which mirrored her ego: scraped, bruised, and bloodied. She made herself comfortable and didn't have any intention on returning to class. If she had her way, she would lock herself in that restroom stall forever.

Chapter 2

You're the queen of the earth, there's a throne waitin' for you/
They might as well diss their own mother if they hatin' on you/

The bell rang, and students scattered out of the classroom and jammed into the hall. Mahogany dragged through the halls of Bronx High with the added baggage of the not-so-flattering self-portrait drawn by Nevaeh. She couldn't shake the sketch from her mind as she trampled down the stairs to the first floor of the school. The first floor was where the gym, the locker rooms, and some of the specials classes were located, such as dance, culinary arts, and computer science. As she rounded the corner, Mahogany was greeted by a horde of boys who were hanging out by the boys' restroom, a popular spot for the class cutters.

Mahogany's presence in the hall caught the attention of the boys slouching against the wall. Just as Mahogany lifted her chin, pinned her shoulders back, and began to strut, the boys averted their attention to the other side of the hall. Mahogany followed their eyes and spotted Nevaeh and Nyla, strutting toward her from the opposite end. She sneered at the limelight-stealing twins. They weren't *really* twins, but both of them had identical hair weaves and matching stink attitudes.

The *twins* strutted, shoulder to shoulder, blushing at each bark, groan, and invitation from the boys to join them in the restroom. As the *twins* approached Mahogany, their eyes locked in on each other.

"Look, its Soy Sauce," Nevaeh chuckled, pointing at Mahogany.

"Excuse me!" Mahogany snapped, stopping in her tracks.

"You heard what she said!" Nyla jumped in. "Are you mad or nah?!"

Waves of anger surged through Mahogany's body, causing her to tremble in her stance. Her slight overbite clamped down on her bottom lip and gnawed, feverishly. Mahogany's hands curled into tight fists, fingernails digging into her palms. Instead of her fists firing into the smug faces of Nevaeh and Nyla, Mahogany fired words instead. "Ya mother!"

"What?!" Nevaeh shrieked.

"You heard me. I said ya mother!" Mahogany repeated, venom in her voice. Nevaeh and Nyla glared angrily at Mahogany as she turned and started up the hall. Mahogany didn't get far. Pain erupted from the back of her head, and Mahogany crumbled to the floor at the feet of Nevaeh and

Nyla. Pathetic moans escaped from Mahogany's mouth while her body curled up like an injured mutt. Through blurred vision, Mahogany saw Nyla hovering over her, clutching a thick textbook.

The boys removed their backs from the walls and surrounded the girls, pumping their fists and chanting, "Girl fight! Girl fight!" All of a sudden, the sleepy halls roared to life like fight night in Vegas.

While Mahogany's eyes were following the back-and-forth dance of the textbook like a cobra charmer, an arm slithered under her chin, wrapped around her throat, and squeezed the air out of her windpipe. Both of Mahogany's hands tried to rip the arm from around her neck, and her body tried to squirm away from the death grip. "Don'tchu ever in ya little black life talk about my mother again!" Nevaeh screamed in Mahogany's ear, tightening her grip around her neck.

While this was going on, Nyla grabbed a handful of Mahogany's hair and yanked and pulled as if she were trying to tear her ponytail from her scalp. Mahogany jerked her neck forward as she and Nyla engaged in a game of tug of war, using Mahogany's ponytail as the rope. Nyla gave one last tug, stumbled backward, and fell to the seat of her jeans with pieces of the *rope* in her fists. Mahogany's scalp was on fire. Her yelps of pain were caught in her windpipe, between her throat and the crowbar grip of Nevaeh's arm.

Mahogany was feeling lightheaded. Her arms were flailing and her feet were kicking wildly, as if she were submerged under water. She felt like she was drowning. Couldn't breathe. Mahogany's lady lumps were gyrating and bouncing underneath her chin.

The boys were animals, chanting, "Take it off! Take it off!" Nyla grabbed two fistfuls of Mahogany's blue button-down shirt and tugged and pulled until the top buttons popped off. Mahogany's pink bra was showing. The wolf pack behind the girls howled and surrounded them like fresh prey.

Air. Stale hallway air. It never felt so good to breathe. The arm loosened its grip and slithered away from her neck. Mahogany rolled over on her back, her mouth wide and her nostrils flared, swallowing as much air as she could. To Mahogany's surprise, a big girl was yanking Nyla off of her after tossing Nevaeh aside.

The first warning bell blared through the halls. The wolf pack stumbled into the boys' restroom, and Nevaeh and Nyla took off running down the hall. Mahogany pinched her shirt closed and accepted the girl's extended hand.

"You a'ight?" the girl asked, pulling Mahogany to her feet. Mahogany nodded, tears forming in her eyes as she was led into the girls' restroom.

"You look familiar," Mahogany said, studying the girl's face. "Ain't you in my English class?"

"Yeah, I sit in the back. The reason why you hardly recognize me is because I normally skip that class. And when I do decide to show up, I usually fall asleep. First period is way too early in the morning for me."

"Tell me about it," Mahogany agreed. "So, what's your name again?"

"Karisma."

"Oh yeah. Wasn't Ms. Yeager messing up your name on the first day of school?"

"Teachers always mispronouncing my name and be having me ready to punch somebody's child in the face because students think it's funny when they mess up my name. Ka-ris-ma! What's so hard about that?"

Mahogany bent over the sink and splashed water on her face. She turned sideways in the mirror to get a look at what was left of her ponytail. More tears raced across Mahogany's face and mingled with the faucet water splashes.

"It's really not that bad. It looks like most of the hair broke from the middle and not the scalp." Karisma shrugged. Mahogany glared at Karisma as she dried her face. Seeing that Mahogany wasn't amused, Karisma added, "Even if Nyla managed to yank ya whole ponytail off, you would still have more hair than her. Trust me, I seen her before she got that Brazilian hair weave. She ain't working with much."

Mahogany wasn't sure if Karisma was lying or trying to make her laugh. She figured it was the latter. Mahogany glanced at the black headscarf that hid Karisma's hair from view and wondered how much *she* was working with. Karisma always hid her hair under a headscarf. And in the back of their English class, she would fold her arms on the desk, forming a nest, and hide her face in it. Snores and whistles would escape from the nest just to let everyone know how bored she was. Even when she wasn't snoring, her round-Hershey face would often face the floor when she spoke. Mahogany never understood why she hid her face; she wasn't an ugly girl by any means.

Karisma was a big girl. Not fat, just big. Or rather, thick. And tall. She stood about five feet seven, and her dress attire, usually jeans and tan suede Timberland boots, made most people think she was a tomboy. She had the coaches chasing her up and down the school hallways, trying to convince her to play on the girls' basketball team.

Karisma leaned against one of the stalls, occasionally glancing at her iPhone, while Mahogany took a seat on the sink and pinched her shirt closed with her index finger and thumb.

"Why did you help me?" Mahogany asked curiously.

"Dag, girl! You say that like you ain't want no help. If I didn't help you when I did, you would be bald-headed like Mr. Abraham right now, the way that girl was pulling out ya hair. And not only that, but you would be layin' in the middle of the hall snoring louder than I do in Ms. Yeager's class. She had you in the crazy sleeper hold." Mahogany wasn't sure why, but that comment tickled the heck out of her. Laughter detonated from Mahogany's core. Karisma joined her as laughs echoed throughout the restroom.

"My bad, it's just that...we've never said a word to each other before," Mahogany said, still coughing out chuckles.

"An enemy of my friend is a friend...no wait...a friend of my enemy is an enemy, or something like that."

"I don't think you're saying it right."

"You know what I mean."

"So are you sayin' you don't like them girls either?"

"Can't stand them. They walk around like they don't bleed every month like the rest of us chicks." Mahogany blushed. Karisma continued, "Fareal, and they so fake. They be smilin' in ya face, then be dissin' you behind ya back. I been waitin' for a reason to put hands on Nevaeh and Nyla. So what happened? Why are you beefin' wit' them?"

"They drew a picture of me on a piece of paper, making me look as black as tar. Then, when they walked past me a few minutes ago, they called me Soy Sauce. I turned to one of 'em and said 'ya mother.' And then...it was *on*."

"They actually drew a picture of you on a piece of paper like some third-graders? Who does that?" Mahogany shook her head as Karisma paused to check her iPhone.

"Yo! Them chicks already runnin' their mouths on the 'gram!" Karisma bellowed.

"Whatchu talking about?" Mahogany asked.

"Nevaeh and Nyla!" Karisma yelled at her iPhone. "They on Instagram right now, talkin' boutchu. Look!" Karisma held up her iPhone and approached Mahogany so she could see for herself what Nevaeh and Nyla wrote about her.

Mahogany squinted while looking at the iPhone and read out loud, "We just beat up some dark-skinned chick. Light-skinned girls stay winning. #teamlightskin."

"Yo, wait till I see them fake-ass light-skinned...oh, my bad. I don't mean to be cursin' in front of you like this," Karisma apologized.

"Why are you apologizing?"

"Ain't you a Jehovah's Witness or somethin'?"

"Yeah. How did you know?"

"Because when Ms. Yeager tried to have that lame Christmas party, I remember you said you don't celebrate Christmas and you left the class."

"Jehovah's Witnesses ain't the only ones who don't celebrate Christmas."

"Yeah, I know. But I know you're not a Muslim, and you damn sure don't look like ya Jewish." They laughed. "So where did you go when you left the class during the party?" Karisma asked.

"The library. Bored outta my mind."

"What other holidays don't y'all celebrate?"

"None of 'em. Easter, Thanksgiving, national holidays, birthdays—"

"—Dag, y'all can't celebrate birthdays?"

"Nope. Well, we're not supposed to."

"There's one question I always wanted to ask a Jehovah's Witness?"

"Yeah, yeah, yeah, I know: Why do we knock on people's doors?"

"That's it! That's the question! How did you know?"

"Whenever someone says they want to ask me a question, *that's* usually the question."

"So what's the answer?"

"It says in the Book of Matthew to go forth and preach to the nations. We arm ourselves with the sword of truth, the Bible, and we go out and preach the good news."

"It don't hurt y'all's feelings when people slam doors in ya faces?"

"It's not supposed to hurt our feelings. We're just trying to give people the opportunity to learn the truth. When people are ready, I guess they will listen." Mahogany slid down off the sink and looked at her hair again in the mirror.

"I can do ya hair for you if you want," Karisma suggested. "I got some hair in my closet." Confusion wrinkled Mahogany's face as she studied Karisma's headscarf again. *What does she know about doing hair?* Mahogany thought.

"Just because I rarely do my own hair doesn't mean I don't know how to do hair." *Oh snap, she's listening to my thoughts.* "What? I never said that you didn't know how to do hair."

"But the look on ya face did."

"My mother always said that I should never play poker because my thoughts and emotions are always written all over my face." Mahogany chuckled. "My bad."

"It's all good. There are plenty of girls walking through the halls of this school with braids by Karisma. My homegirl Kesha, this girl named Noni—"

"Noni?! You mean that skinny quiet girl who hardly ever talks to anybody?"

"Yeah, that's her."

"The box braids you did for her are really nice. You think you can hook my hair up like that?"

"Actually, she has two-strand twists. I don't have enough hair for that, but I can hook you up with some cornrows." The late bell startled them when it rang out.

"Come wit' me to the counselor's office so we can get late passes," Karisma urged.

"How we gon' get late passes from Ms. Camara when we wasn't in her office?"

"She's my second mom; she'll give em' to us. Trust me."

It took two minutes for Karisma and Mahogany to arrive at Ms. Camara's tiny office. Piles of red folders were stacked high on her cluttered desk. Only Ms. Camara's mocha face and loose curly afro were visible.

"Hey, Second Mom?" Karisma called out, hugging Ms. Camara.

"What are you doing here, Karisma? Shouldn't you be in class?"

"See, what had happened was…um…I was on my way to class and then I ran into my homegirl over there, who I haven't seen in a long time. We started talking and catching up and the next thing you know, the late bell rings." Ms. Camara glanced at Mahogany. With concern in her voice she asked, "What happened to your shirt?"

"I popped the buttons playing basketball in gym," Mahogany lied. The expression on Ms. Camara's face spoke to Mahogany. It said, *I don't believe you.* But the stack of red folders and the ringing phone spoke louder to Ms. Camara.

They said, *I don't have time to press the issue right now.* "Hey, I'm on my way," Ms. Camara said into the phone receiver before slipping it back onto the cradle.

"What is your name, young lady?" Ms. Camara asked, returning her attention back to Mahogany.

"Mahogany."

"Mahogany what?"

"Mahogany Brown."

"When my schedule clears up, I will make an appointment for you so we can talk." *Oh my God, she knows,* Mahogany thought as Ms. Camara's piercing eyes were seemingly staring through her. Through her lies, her forced smile, and into her soul, making her spirit uncomfortable. "Talk about what?" A smile etched across Ms. Camara's lips, mirroring the false smile Mahogany wore. "Your classes for next semester." Ms. Camara's eyes moved across Mahogany's face and froze on her right cheek. "Okay."

Ms. Camara handed Mahogany an old shirt from the lost and found box. And just as Karisma promised, she gave the girls late passes, but not before warning Karisma that *that* would be the last time.

Chapter 3

You're wrapped in a beautiful sheet of golden-brown ebony skin/
a mix of mocha and macchiato, a Starbucks-style heavenly blend/

Mahogany was the first one to reach her apartment after school. Beat her older sister, Melani, by three minutes. Mahogany needed every one of those one hundred and eighty seconds. She combed her hair back, tied it down with her blue scarf, and buried the shirt with the missing buttons at the bottom of the hamper. Before she could slip on her nightgown, Melani burst through the front door.

"I was waiting for you after school. Where were you?" Melani asked, half out of breath.

"Um, I really had to go to the bathroom, so, um, I ran home."

"What happened to your face?"

Mahogany threw her arms up, hiding half of her face with her hands as she peeked over her fingers. "What?! What's wrong with my face?" Mahogany asked.

"You have a welt along your right cheek." Mahogany took off running down the hall. She stumbled into the bathroom and stuck her face in front of the mirror. Melani stuck her face in the doorway.

"Why did you change your shirt?" Melani asked. "You weren't wearing that shirt when you left for school this morning. Why did you change it?"

"Oh...because—"

"Were you fighting or something?"

"No, I wasn't fighting."

"It looks like somebody scratched you."

"Nobody scratched me," Mahogany lied, her finger skating across the welt on her cheek. The same cheek that Ms. Camara had fixed her eyes on. Melani stood before her sister, studying her body language to see if she could interpret the lie in Mahogany's facial expressions. Melani frowned, and her narrow eyes sank and nearly disappeared between her high cheekbones and low brows. She was just as brown as their mom, but not quite as brown as Mahogany. With her fingers combing through her bob, Melani studied Mahogany's face and examined her eyebrows.

"I can tell that you are lying to me, Mahogany."

"How can you tell?"

"Whenever you lie, your eyebrows twitch," Melani revealed, her eyes seesawing from Mahogany's eyes to her eyebrows, waiting for a response.

"Nothing happened. Just mind your business."

"Something happened to you at school. If you just tell me, maybe I can help you."

Tired of the interrogation, Mahogany warned, "I need to pee, so watch ya face!" Mahogany slammed the door on her nose and waited until she heard Melani walk down the hall. Then she slipped into her room and waited on Mom. Mahogany knew Melani was going to tell Mom about her face. It's what she did.

Mahogany wasn't too worried about Mom though. She was predictable. Mom would ask the same questions Melani asked, and Mahogany would offer her the same bowl of *bull* that she fed to her sister, and she would do this while trying to keep her eyebrows from jumping. Mom might grow a little suspicious, and then she would grow more tired because it was a work night.

Work days and nights were long and tiring for Mom. Not only because she sat in a cubicle in somebody's office, but also because she traveled back and forth to and from Downtown Manhattan. Each morning she would drive and park at the train station and take the number five train downtown to work. After work, she took the five train back Uptown, got into her car, and would reach home close to seven each evening. She would be too tired to drill

Mahogany about what really happened in school, so she wasn't too worried.

Behind the privacy of her locked bedroom door, Mahogany sat in front of her dresser mirror and carefully removed the headscarf from her head. Her eyes traced the hair of the girl in the mirror. Without warning or special request, the chorus to the song that was stuck in her head rang out again…*You so black…You so black…You so black*! Her face began to twitch from sadness and her eyes swam behind pools of tears. Mahogany cursed under her breath, upset that she was about to cry again. Before the bitter pools streamed from her eyes and emptied into the corners of her mouth, she snatched her face away from the mirror. She rewrapped the scarf around her head, grabbed her phone, and searched Google for skin-bleaching creams. If only her skin were as light as Malikah's.

The selections were overwhelming, and after reading several reviews on select skin-bleaching creams, she decided to continue her search another time.

Mahogany grabbed her drawing pad and pencil from the bed and took a seat on the cold radiator in front of the window. She placed the drawing pad on her lap and twirled the pencil between her fingers like a mini baton. While the street noise kept her ears company, her eyes traced the outlines of the noisemakers. She placed the lead on the paper and lost herself on the blank page as the pencil sketched the scene on the other side of her window.

Mahogany had been drawing since she was three. When she was a toddler, she drew what she saw, which was mainly cartoon characters. But as she matured, so did her drawings. On the pages of her drawing pad, Miss Piggy no longer wore pink dresses and held lollypops; she now wore retro Jordans and hoop earrings and posed as if taking a selfie on the street corner. Miss Piggy's facial features changed as well. Her pink skin tanned to an acorn brown, her snout morphed into the burly nose of Queen Nefertiti, and her lips were pouty and lip-glossy moist. The new Miss Piggy covered many pages in her drawing pad and could have easily been mistaken for one of Mahogany's individual class pictures in the photo albums on the coffee table in the living room.

Not only did Mahogany's drawings mature, but sitting in front of the television watching cartoons no longer held Mahogany's attention. The window showing twenty-four-hour coverage of the thugs and thug-divas on the corner was much more entertaining. Mahogany would watch the same channel day and night. And her pencil captured the life outside of her window and immortalized it in her drawing pad. Sketches of low- and high-rise red-brick buildings, of liquor stores and light-skinned girls snuggled in the arms of the corner thugs posing in front of the light poles. If Mahogany could see it from her window, she sketched it. She had more drawings of the ghetto on her wall than James Evans Jr. had in his living room.

Mahogany peered absently through the window as the day faded away. As did the screams of playing kids who scrambled toward the safety of their apartments and away from the approaching darkness. While her classmates sat in front of their televisions, probably mesmerized by late-night hip-hop wives reality shows, Mahogany's face remained as still as a picture in the frame of her window until the streetlights glistened in her ebony eyes, watching the real reality show just below her window.

Huddled beneath the streetlight were a bunch of chocolate-faced dudes with what looked like a caramel center in their group. Before long, some of the thugs broke apart like a Reese's candy bar, exposing the three peanut-butter-faced girls that were posing in the middle.

The thugs laughed with them, bobbed their heads to music with them, play-fought with them, and begged for hugs from them. As darkness ate away the remaining pieces of daylight, the thugs wrapped their arms around the necks of the girls, and they disappeared into the night until only two remained. Mahogany raised the window as high as it could go and stuck her head between the height of the window guards and the opened window. She didn't know the girl, but the boy looked very familiar. They were shoulder to shoulder and hand in hand as their backs rested against the red bricks of her building.

"Come on, girl, lemme taste them luscious lips," the boy begged, puckering his lips and leaning toward the girl.

"No, not out here." The girl blushed, shoving the boy back.

"A'ight then, let's go to my apartment."

"You know I can't do that."

"Why not?"

"I'm not ready. I told you that before."

"I don't understand why we gotta wait."

"I just want to make sure this is real. I want to make sure you really love me."

"I tell you I luh you all the time. Listen, I luh you. See."

"I believe you, but if you really love me, you'd wait on me." The boy's body deflated against the wall. His fingers went limp in the girl's hand. He took his hand back and gave her a half hug before walking across the street to the building directly across from Mahogany's.

"Makai! Wait! Makai!" the girl called out. Makai ignored her pleas and stormed into his building.

He looks so familiar, Mahogany mumbled to herself. About a minute later, the third-floor window directly across from hers stood out amongst the other obscure windows. That window didn't just stand out because it was the only window on that building, radiating light as if the sun had climbed down from the sky and went to bed for the night behind it. It stood out because of the boy who was now sitting behind the window. *It was him.* It was Mahogany's *window boyfriend.*

About a month ago, like clockwork, his face would appear in his window almost at the same time as Mahogany's would. About fifteen minutes after three, as soon as both of them arrived home from school, Makai's face would appear behind the bars of his window guards. Mahogany was certain that Makai's eyes were fixed on the corner thugs who were guarding the *corner* from other young thugs from other *corners* of the projects. From her window seat, Mahogany witnessed many young thugs wander too far from their corners and stumble onto the corner across the street from her window. She and Makai watched as the lost thugs got their pockets dug for loose change and then had guns aimed at their faces until they retreated back to their own corners.

While Mahogany would wince and turn her eyes away from the corner attacks, she noticed Makai's eyes jumping with curious excitement. Before long, his face was snatched from the frame of his window like an old photo. For months, the light behind his window went dark and the curtains were closed as if the window show were over. It wasn't until that night that Mahogany discovered Makai had moved his show to the other side of his window. He'd become one of the corner boys.

With the exception of Makai and his window, nothing else seemed to exist. Piece by piece, everything else seemed to fall away: the other windows, the building, the few people outside, and the occasional car that crept down the street. It was just Mahogany, her window peephole, and Makai, her audience of one.

Mahogany's eyes danced around Makai's features while his eyes were locked in on the girl he had just walked away from. His eyes followed her until she rounded the corner. Angrily, he snatched his face from the window and sealed his curtains shut, officially closing his window-eye on Mahogany. She remained in the window, hoping Makai would return, but he didn't. An hour later, Mahogany's face was still in the window, her eyes looking down at her drawing pad. Her pencil continued to recreate the block on the other side of her window. The likeness of every thug's face that was on the block an hour earlier appeared in her drawing pad. But all the girls were omitted. They were replaced by one girl. A girl with a strong resemblance to Mahogany. Except Mahogany's skin was lighter. Whenever Mahogany sketched a portrait of herself in her drawing pad, she would use the earth-tone colored pencil to shade inside the lines. But that night, she used the beige colored pencil to lighten up her skin on the drawing pad, the way she imagined her skin would look once she got ahold of some skin-bleaching cream. In the sketch, all of the thug's eyes were on her. Just the way she imagined it.

Chapter 4

in a world where color matters, it's hard to maintain control/
forgettin' hymns, committin' sins, just to ease the pain in ya soul/

"There's no way I can go inside that school with my hair looking like this!" Mahogany exclaimed, standing several feet in front of the school entrance.

"Girl, you trippin'." Karisma smirked. "I told you yesterday, the pieces of hair that broke off is hardly noticeable. You paranoid right now."

"To you it's not noticeable. But to me—"

"Why don't you just keep ya scarf on?" Karisma cut in. "I never take mine off."

"That's because you don't have Mr. Garrison," Mahogany said. "There's no way he's gonna let me sit in his class with this scarf on my head. He's super strict, and I know he's gonna make me take it off."

"Then come wit' me to my crib."

"When? Now?"

"Yeah. I told you yesterday that I would do ya hair for you. We can chill and watch Netflix while I braid ya hair."

"I don't know. I never skipped school before."

"Ain't nothin' to worry about; you ain't gonna get caught. But if you want, you can always go inside the school, take off ya scarf, and let everyone laugh at ya hairdo that looks more like a *hair-don't*." The girls laughed.

"You sure I'm not gonna get a letter home or a phone call home or somethin'?" Mahogany asked.

"If this is ya first time being absent, nah," Karisma pointed out. "Now, when you reach your tenth time skipping school like me, then you'll start gettin' letters and phone calls."

"You never got in trouble?"

"Nah." Karisma shrugged. "My mom will say 'don't do it again.' I say, 'okay.' And that's the end of it. She don't really care that much." Karisma turned and started in the other direction. She turned her head back toward Mahogany and gave her a look with the eye that wasn't lazy. "So, whassup? You comin' with me or what?" Karisma asked. Mahogany hesitated at first, but eventually turned her back on the school and followed Karisma in the other direction.

Karisma's apartment was just like all the other apartments Mahogany had seen in the projects. As soon as she entered her apartment, she was greeted by a long, obscure hall. The kitchen was on the right and the living room on the left. There were three bedrooms and a bathroom at the end of the hall. The girls made a sharp right at the end of the hall and entered the bathroom, where Karisma washed Mahogany's hair in the tub. After blow-drying Mahogany's hair, Karisma reached into her closet and removed a plastic bag full of packages of hair. She sat on the end of her full-size bed, and Mahogany sat on the floor, between Karisma's legs. Karisma combed out Mahogany's hair with a brown comb and parted the hair, front to back.

"So who else lives here with you?" Mahogany asked as Karisma began braiding the first piece of synthetic hair into Mahogany's hair.

"Just my mom."

"No brothers or sisters?"

"I have an older brother named Caine."

"How much older?"

"He's thirty-eight."

"Thirty-eight?! He's old enough to be your father."

"Facts," Karisma agreed.

"What made your parents have children so far apart?"

"We have different fathers," Karisma explained. "My mom and Caine's dad got married when they were eighteen and nineteen years old. Soon after Caine was born, they divorced. My mom lived the single life for twenty-two years until she met my dad. And that's when I was born."

"Is Caine your brother's real name?

"Caine is his street name. His real name is Cole. Get it! Cole Caine as in cocaine."

"Where's Caine now?"

"Up north."

"Oh, he moved to Canada?"

"Nah," Karisma chuckled. "Up north means he's in prison in Upstate New York. Waaay upstate. Close to Canada."

"Why is your brother locked up?"

"He got caught with drugs."

"Was he a drug user?"

"Nah, my brother was one of the biggest drug dealers in the projects," Karisma stated proudly. "Every hand-to-hand drug dealer in the projects had to go through him and his crew to get drugs to sell. His crew had the projects on lock."

"How long is your brother going to be locked up?"

"Actually, when he and my bae got caught with the drugs, they were supposed to be in there for a long, long time. But my brother said they may be coming home soon. Something about an illegal arrest or evidence tampering or something like that."

"Did you say your bae?"

"Yeah, my boyfriend JoJo used to sell drugs for my brother. But my brother doesn't know that me and one of his boys are seeing each other. If my brother ever finds out…" Karisma slit her throat with her finger.

"Wait a minute," Mahogany said, trying to make sense of what was just said. "Your brother is thirty-eight, and you are going out with one of his boys? How old is he?"

"JoJo is only nineteen years old. Like I said, he was one of my brother's workers."

"Nineteen is still old to you. You're only sixteen."

"I like older guys." Karisma shrugged.

"What does ya dad have to say about you goin' out with a nineteen-year old?"

"Kind of hard to share ya opinion when you're buried six feet under the ground."

"Oh...my bad...I'm sorry. I didn't mean to—"

"Don't stress it. He was dead to us *before* he died. And my mother made sure of that." Karisma changed the subject and put the spotlight on Mahogany. "So, which Cosby kid are *you*?"

"What do you mean?"

"You seem like you come from a good, well-off family. Ya moms is probably a lawyer, ya dad's a doctor, you have brothers and sisters who never get in trouble, y'all go to church every Sunday, and—"

"Since when did the Cosby kids live in the projects?" Mahogany cut in.

"Good one," Karisma laughed.

"But seriously, my mom ain't no lawyer; she's a secretary...or, I mean, an administrative assistant. I don't have any brothers. Only a sister, Melani, who's older by a year."

"And what about ya dad? You sayin' he ain't a doctor?"

"Um...I'm not really supposed to talk about him," Mahogany hesitated.

"Dag, what did ya dad do that was so bad that you can't talk about him?"

"Well, you're not a Jehovah's Witness, so, I guess I can tell you. My dad was disfellowshipped from the Kingdom Hall."

"Disfellowshipped?"

"Kicked out."

"Why, what happened?"

"My mom never told me what he did, but I'm pretty sure he broke one of the rules. That's why he was asked… *told* to leave. When someone is disfellowshipped, all the other Jehovah's Witnesses are not supposed to associate with them."

"Not even family?" Mahogany shook her head. "But that's ya dad, though," Karisma said.

"I know, but, I don't make the rules." Mahogany shrugged.

"That's messed up. Do you get to see him at least?"

"I haven't seen my dad in over two years. I know he stays with my grandmother from time to time. The building right next to the big park. I also heard he spends a lot of time in one of those sports bars on Boston Road."

"The building next to the big park? That's just at the end of the block, about five or six buildings from here. That's not far at all. You need to go see him. The last time I saw my dad, I was so angry with him, and I don't know why. I cursed him out like a dog, and my mother stood behind me, cheering me on. She hated my dad so much that she didn't care that I was cursing. All I know is, ever since I was little, my mom always talked bad about my dad, so I figured I was supposed to hate him. After he died, I started to think about all the times I spent with my dad since I was young, and you know what?"

"What?"

"It wasn't all bad. In fact, it was mostly good. I remember him teaching me how to ride my bike. Taking me out for ice cream. I remember he took me out to a restaurant for dinner and he pulled the chair out for me and everything. No boy ever pulled my chair out for me. Actually, no boy ever took me to a restaurant. Except one time when JoJo took me to the pizza shop. The chairs we sat on while we ate were bolted to the floor, so he couldn't pull it out." The girls laughed together. "All I'm saying is, whatever beef my mom had with my dad had nothing to do with me. Me and my dad's relationship was fine when I was little. Then all of a sudden, he and my mom had a falling out, and my *mom* bans him from the apartment and from seeing us. It wasn't my fight; it was my mom's fight, and I had no reason to be so mad at him. You just never know what the future holds. So spend as much time with your dad while you still can."

"Wow, that's deep, Karisma. Makes me wanna reach out to my dad."

"You should."

"You know, my dad is the only man that told me I was beautiful," Mahogany revealed.

"JoJo is the only dude that ever told me I was pretty. While we were eating pizza, he said, 'You're pretty for a dark-skinned girl.' I slapped him across his face with my hot pizza. He said it as if dark-skinned girls are unattractive and he found it surprising that me, a dark-skinned girl, was pretty."

"What did he do when you slapped him with your pizza?"

"He was about to dive across the table and choke the life outta me until I quickly apologized and wiped the hot cheese off his face with a bunch of napkins."

"You crazy, Karisma," Mahogany laughed. "But seriously, I guess you weren't too hurt by the comments. You're still with him."

"Of course. He's my bae. And regardless, he did say that I was pretty."

"My ex-boyfriend, Tafari, actually told me I was pretty, but his actions told me I still wasn't good enough."

"Whatchu mean?"

"He dumped me for a light-skinned girl."

"Typical," Karisma seethed. "Them light-skinned chicks stay stealing somebody's man. I hate them!"

"Karisma, let me ask you a question?"

"Go 'head."

"You ever thought about using skin-bleaching creams on ya face to make yaself lighter?"

"I thought about it and…I used it."

"You did? Did it work?"

"Does it look like is worked?" Mahogany turned and looked up at Karisma's face. "I'm still as dark as I've always been."

"Maybe you didn't use the right one. Which one did you use?"

"It's on my dresser."

Mahogany rose up and walked over to Karisma's dresser. She examined the skin whitener tone and bleach cream jar. Mahogany twisted off the top and realized it was half gone. "Do you mind if I put some on?" Mahogany asked.

"Go 'head. I don't care," Karisma answered. "Matter of fact, you can have it." Mahogany jabbed two fingers into the jar, rubbed the cream into the palm of her hand, and smeared it all over her face. She stuffed the jar into her backpack before making her way back over to Karisma so she could finish her hair.

Three hours later, Karisma was done, and she covered Mahogany's braids with a cloud of coconut hairspray. Mahogany's cornrows went straight back and extended down to the middle of her back. She climbed to her feet, stretched like she was yawning, and kicked the kinks out of her legs. Mahogany stuck her face in the dresser mirror and almost didn't recognize the girl staring back. Whoever she was, she smiled, and that was a first because her reflection never flashed her straight-whites at Mahogany. It didn't take long to figure out why. Mahogany's new 'do made her face look...not so bad. Or, was it the bleaching cream? Was it working already?

Karisma gathered the braids from Mahogany's back and dunked the ends into a pot of boiling hot water. She told Mahogany the hot water would keep the ends of the braids from unraveling.

"Wow, you look like a different person," Karisma declared. "You got ya hair *did*, now, you need some new clothes."

"What's wrong with my clothes?"

"Come on, chick, look at yaself." Karisma chuckled. "Khakis, a white button-up, and them shoes. You look like you got dressed for church this morning, not for school."

"I do have a pair of jeans at home, but they're dirty."

"Did you say *a* pair of jeans? As in *one* pair of jeans?" Mahogany nodded. "I *can't* witchu right now." Karisma laughed. She doubled over, clutching her stomach as if she'd been kicked in the gut. "That's it, we're going to the mall and I'm taking you shopping," Karisma declared.

"Shopping?" Mahogany parroted. "I ain't got no shopping money."

"Don't worry about it. I gotchu." The right side of Karisma's body disappeared in her closet as she picked a pair of blue jeans off of a hanger.

"Go into my bathroom, take off your khakis, and put these jeans on," Karisma requested, tossing a pair of baggy jeans at Mahogany.

"Why?"

"You'll be more comfortable."

"But I don't understand."

"Just trust me on this. Plus, do you really wanna go hang out at the mall with those khakis on?"

Mahogany did as Karisma requested. She entered the bathroom and changed into the baggy jeans.

It was a five-minute walk to the bus stop, a ten-minute wait for the bus, and a twenty-five-minute ride to the Galleria at White Plains Mall. The Galleria, a popular hangout spot for teens especially on weekends, was located in the city of White Plains, which was a part of Westchester County, a suburb just north of the Bronx.

Upon entering the mall, the girls went straight to the food court and ordered two dulce de leche milkshakes from Haagen-Dazs. “This is my first time in this mall,” Mahogany revealed, straw to her lips, sipping her milkshake.

“Are you serious?” Karisma asked, disbelief in her voice. “If I’m not at Bay Plaza, I come up here all the time just to hang out and kick it.”

“I don’t know if I could come up here too often. That bus ride is too long.”

“Yeah, I feel you,” Karisma agreed. “It is a long bus ride. That’s why the last couple of times I came up here, my homegirl Ya Ya drove us.”

The girls window-shopped until they finished their milkshakes. Afterwards, Karisma led Mahogany into a clothing store. “I never seen a mall so empty,” Mahogany said, browsing through a rack of jeans.

“Who do you expect to be in here?” Karisma asked rhetorically. “It’s during school and work hours.”

“Yeah, I know,” Mahogany said. “I like it better like this, though. No long lines to wait on. No crowds of people bumping into you or just in your way at every turn.”

“I hate it when the mall is empty.”

“Why?”

“It’s harder to shop. But we gon’ do this anyway.”

“Why is it harder? And do *what* anyway?” Mahogany asked, confusion in her voice and on her face.

"You like these jeans?" Karisma asked, ignoring Mahogany's question.

"Look at the price. They're too expensive."

"I ain't ask you all that. Do you like 'em?"

"Heck yeah. The jeans are fly, but—"

"A'ight then. Find ya size, get about three pairs in the same color, and follow me to the dressing room." Mahogany draped three pairs of the jeans across her arm and followed Karisma toward the back of the store. One of the workers, a thin Puerto Rican girl who looked like she was playing hooky from high school herself, showed them to the dressing rooms in the back corner. Once in the dressing room, Mahogany wiggled into a pair of the blue jeans. She stepped out of the dressing room and posed in front of the floor-to-ceiling mirror that was to the immediate right.

Mahogany turned to the left and right, eyes sizing up her body from all angles. "I'm lovin' the way my booty looks in these jeans," Mahogany beamed, eyes gleaming as Karisma joined her in front of the mirror.

"Now you look like someone that I can hag wit'," Karisma joked. "So, you *feelin'* them jeans or what?"

"I love them," Mahogany cheered. "I can't take my eyes off my reflection. It's almost like it's a different person staring back at me. The braids...these jeans...I feel like a brand new person." Karisma scanned the area and inched closer to Mahogany. "When you go back into the dressing room, don't take those jeans off. Just put the baggy jeans on top of the jeans that you're wearing. Then, bring the other jeans back out and meet me right here."

Clouds of confusion that had formed in Mahogany's mind when she arrived at the mall were clearing up. It finally dawned on her that Karisma's idea of *shopping* was *stealing*.

"I-I don't know about this," Mahogany stammered, her stomach turning.

"Don't know about what?"

"Stealing," Mahogany whispered. "It just doesn't feel right."

"Whatchu mean it don't feel right?" Karisma huffed. "Don't you feel good about ya self in them jeans? You just said you feel like a brand new person. But if you don't *know about this,* then take them jeans off, put them back on the rack over there, put ya khakis on, and you can go back to being ya old self." Karisma's words fired from her mouth like fists, hitting Mahogany in her gut and rocking her deep to her moral core. In her gut, Mahogany knew the jeans should go back on the rack, but in her eyes, seeing the way the jeans caressed her curvy hips, it seemed as though every stitch in the jeans were designed just for her thighs. A quick glance to admire her reflection and another look of assurance from Karisma convinced Mahogany to do something she had never done before. Ignore her gut.

First it was fighting, then cutting class, and now stealing. Page by page, Mahogany was losing the morals she'd learned from her mom and in the Kingdom Hall. But in that moment, it didn't matter. All that mattered was the girl with the long, neat braids and the skin-tight jeans staring back at her from the mirror. She couldn't wait to reveal her at school.

Mahogany stepped out of the dressing room with the baggy jeans pulled over the jeans she'd tried on, the remaining two pairs draped over her arm.

"Follow me," Karisma said to Mahogany as they approached the young worker.

"Did you ladies find anything that you liked?" the young worker asked.

"The jeans are cool and all, but they don't fit right," Karisma said. Mahogany handed the worker the extra jeans.

"If you don't like these, we just got some new jeans that came in yesterday. Do you want to look at them?" the girl asked.

"Nah, maybe some other time. We're just gonna walk around the mall for a little while. Thank you, though." Karisma and Mahogany headed for the door. Mahogany's heart was pounding in excitement as she and Karisma approached the entrance. *We're actually gonna get away with this*, Mahogany thought. As soon as those words danced across her brain, the metal detectors started beeping when they crossed the entrance's threshold. The ear-ringing, repetitive beeps confused Mahogany, causing her to freeze at the entrance. To Karisma, however, the *beeping* might as well have been a shot from a starter pistol the way she took off running. "Come on, let's go!" Karisma barked at Mahogany, turning over her shoulder as she ran. Karisma's voice snapped Mahogany out of her brief fog, and she dashed out of the store. An explosion of static startled Mahogany as she ran through the mall. She looked over her shoulder and saw a mall security guard chasing behind her while screaming for back-up into his walkie-talkie.

"This way!" Karisma called out before making a sharp right and running through the food court. The girls were dodging and weaving around mall shoppers with two security guards now in hot pursuit. "Over here!" Karisma called out as both girls burst through the fire exists.

Nervous panting while they ran through the mall turned into giggling relief once they reached the safety of the outdoors. The running slowed to a jog, then to a fast walk as they put three blocks between them and the Galleria. They keeled over by the bus stop, sucking wind like asthmatics.

"Oh, my God!" Mahogany chuckled nervously. "It feels like my heart is about to burst through my chest."

"Feels good, don't it?" Karisma asked, a crazed look in her bright eyes. "I love this feeling. When the adrenaline is pumping like this."

"Only feels good because we didn't get caught. I can't believe you ran and left me at the entrance."

"Why the heck did you freeze up like that?"

"That beeping caught me off guard. I was confused for a second."

"Didn't you know the metal detectors were gonna beep? I mean, you have on a pair of stolen jeans with the tags still on 'em?"

"I totally forgot about the tags. For some reason, I thought we were just gonna walk out of the store with no problems."

"It's a good thing you snapped out of it. If you didn't, they would have caught you and they would have held you until ya moms came and picked you up."

"That wouldn't have been good at all."

"But, we didn't get caught, so now it's all good." Karisma hiked up her sweatshirt to give Mahogany a glimpse of what was underneath.

"You stole the shirt you were looking at in the store?" Mahogany gasped.

"You think I didn't when I *did*?" Karisma smiled. "Actually, I stole two shirts. One for me and one for you."

"One for me?"

"Yeah." Karisma hiked up the shirt underneath her sweatshirt, revealing a third shirt. "You needed a shirt to match ya new jeans, right?"

"You're crazy," Mahogany laughed. "Ya boobs is waaay bigger than mine. I don't wear the same size as you, so how am I gonna be able to fit that shirt?"

"Who says this is my size?" Karisma asked. "I can barely breathe in this shirt. Now I know how my grandmother feels when she be wearing them Spanx."

"If that's my shirt, take it off before you stretch it out more than it is."

"You want me to strip right here at the bus stop?" Karisma asked. Mahogany glanced at the boy sitting on the bench a few feet from the bus stop and cracked, "I'm sure *he* wouldn't mind." She laughed.

"Yo, whatchu say?!" Karisma snapped at the boy sitting on the bench.

"Whatchu talkin' 'bout?" the boy snapped back.

"Karisma, what happened?" Mahogany asked.

"That dude said something slick about me!"

"You must be paranoid or something! I ain't say nothin' 'boutchu! I don't even know you!"

"I saw you!" Karisma barked back. "You were looking over here and you were mumbling something!"

"You know what?" the boy asked rhetorically as he stood from the bench. "I'mma walk over to the other bus stop because if I stay here, I'mma catch one of dem domestic violence charges today."

"Yo, you talkin' real reckless right now!" Karisma barked, flinching at the boy as if she were going to punch him. "You better keep walking!"

"Chill, Karisma," Mahogany said, grabbing Karisma by the arm. "Let him go!" Mahogany waited until the boy crossed the street before she took off the baggy jeans and discarded them into the nearby trashcan. Mahogany and Karisma ripped off all the tags just before the bus arrived. Mahogany rode home on the bus with new jeans, new braids, and new confidence.

Chapter 5

You're a queen, a daughter, a sister, an artist, a leader/
an angel, a goddess, a provider, a healer, a teacher/

Mahogany and Karisma got off the bus just minutes before the high school students were to be dismissed for the day. "Come with me to my apartment so I can give you ya shirt," Karisma urged.

"I can't," Mahogany said. "I need to go back to the school so I can meet up with my sister."

"Why can't you just meet her at ya apartment?"

"My mom likes for us to walk home from school together. If I don't meet her in front of the school, she's gonna suspect that I played hooky, and I don't want her to know."

"Um, I got some bad news for you," Karisma said, sarcasm in her voice. "Last time ya sister saw you, which was before school, you had on an old scarf and a pair of khakis. Now, it's after school, and she's gonna see you in a pair of new jeans and a new hairdo. Unless you can convince her that we have a beauty class in school, she's gonna know you skipped."

"Oh, yeah," Mahogany said, hiding her face in shame as if she'd just beamed down from the planet of the stupids. "I guess I didn't think this all the way through, huh?"

"I don't see why you just can't tell her," Karisma said. "Me and my brother used to keep secrets from our parents all the time. You ever heard the sayin', 'Am I my brother's keeper'?"

"Yeah, my sister is my *keeper,* all right," Mahogany mocked. "Always managing to keep me in trouble. Ever since we were little. I can still hear my mother now: '*Who spilled juice on my rug?!*' Melani would say, '*Mahogany did it!*' Then Mom would call out, '*Who was messing in my makeup?!*' Melani would call back, '*Mahogany did it!*' I remember one time, Mom was in her room. She was upset and she yelled, '*Who did...*' and before she could finish her sentence, Melani yelled, '*Mahogany!*'"

"You crazy, girl," Karisma laughed.

"I never had any type of relationship with my sister," Mahogany revealed. "I always imagined most sisters and brothers shared toys and secrets, kinda like you and your brother did. But we never did that. At times, it felt like I was an only child, and Melani and my mother were sisters. While I played by myself, Melani played guessing games with Mom. '*Guess what Mahogany told me?*' Melani would say to Mom right after I told her a secret. I may have Mom's eyes, but Melani has Mom's ears, literally. That's why I can't tell her anything."

"Well, you better think of something to tell her, quick. School should be lettin' out any minute now," Karisma said, checking the time on her iPhone.

"Oh, snap, thanks for reminding me," Mahogany said. "I'll catch you tomorrow, Karisma. Later."

On her walk back to the school, Mahogany thought about what she was going to say to Melani. Mahogany was trying to figure out how she would explain her hair growing ten inches since the time they walked to school in the morning to the time they met up in the afternoon. Not only did it grow, but it miraculously twisted into neat cornrows. As she walked, excuses and lies ran tireless laps in her mind, but none of them made any sense. Telling Melani the truth made the *most* sense, but it certainly wasn't the *best* sense.

When Mahogany reached the school, her cheeks were puffed with lies that she planned to spew in Melani's ear. By the time she spotted Melani waiting by the entrance, the lies didn't make much sense anymore, so she rinsed them out and let the truth about her hair and new jeans soak into her tongue.

Melani charged at Mahogany and threw her finger in her face. "You didn't have those braids in your hair this morning. How did you get your hair braided? And where did you get them jeans?" Melani asked.

Mahogany swallowed. Not the truth, but air and saliva. "All right, look." Mahogany sighed, readying herself to set the truth free. "I need you to promise me that you're not gonna tell Mom."

"What…I..."

"Promise me!"

"All right, I won't tell," Melani promised, rolling her eyes.

"I played hooky today."

"What! You skipped school?!"

"I had to. I needed to get my hair done."

"Why couldn't you just wait to get it done after school?"

"I wasn't goin' in that building with my hair lookin' the way it did."

"What was wrong with your hair?"

"You were right about the scratch on my face," Mahogany sighed. "I got into a fight yesterday."

"You were fighting? I knew it!"

"Well, it wasn't really a fight. Actually, I got jumped."

"You got jumped and you didn't tell Mom?"

"And you're not gon' tell her either. Just, don't worry 'bout it. It's over with."

"Why did they jump you?"

"They were making fun of me and the way I looked and I didn't like it so I said something back, and that's when they jumped me. And while they were beating me up, one of them grabbed my hair and pulled some of it out."

"So that's why you wore that scarf to school?" Melani asked.

"Yeah."

"So, who did your hair for you?" Melani asked, running her fingers along one of her braids.

"My friend, Karisma," Mahogany answered, knocking Melani's hand away from her hair. "Watch the hair, I just got it done."

"How come I never met her?"

"I just met her yesterday. She saved me while I was getting jumped. I can't imagine what kind of shape I would be in if it wasn't for her."

"You know what? I'm not even shocked that you were fighting and that you played hooky today."

"Why not?"

"You were always kind of a risk-taker. Mom would say do *this*, and you would do *that*. Mom would say *no* and you would say *yes*. Sometimes I used to wish I had as much courage as you. I guess I was a little jealous at times."

"Was it the jealousy that made you tell on me *all* the time?"

"I didn't *always* tell on you."

"Melani, please! You tell every-dag-on-thing!"

"So what about them hooker jeans you're wearing?" Melani asked, changing the subject.

"Hooker jeans?!"

"Them jeans are so tight, I bet your legs are turning blue."

"You don't know what you're talking about. All the girls wear fitted jeans like this."

"Well, all the girls ain't got a mother like ours. When she finds out you're wearing them tight jeans, she's gonna whip you with a strap, right across the back of your legs."

"She's not going to find out. Right?" Mahogany asked, glaring at her sister.

"I'm not going to say anything." She didn't sound very convincing, but Mahogany took her at her word.

When the girls reached their building, a gang of thugs crowded the entrance. Mahogany squeezed by and was attacked by hands. Light brown ones, dark brown ones, ashy ones, fat ones, all reaching from tattered jacket sleeves, grabbing and squeezing Mahogany's hands and arms and her sister's hands and her arms. Melani stiffened her arms as if she were flexing her muscles and yanked them away from their clutches. Mahogany's arms relaxed and allowed the hands to squeeze, grab, and feel. One of the boys' hands tightened around Mahogany's forearm and reeled her into his body. The scent of weed plunged into her nostrils as her nose smashed against his black jacket. She looked into the boy's sleepy eyes, nearly hidden beneath the brim of his black Yankee hat. His face was as brown as the Swisher Sweets blunt tucked behind the crease of his ear. She recognized him instantly. It was Makai, the boy whose window faced hers in the building directly across the street.

"Whassup, Ma? Lemme holla atchew for a minute," Makai said with a sincere smile. Melani grabbed Mahogany's other forearm and tugged, trying to rescue her. "Come on, Mahogany, we have to go."

"Who's that?" Makai asked, tugging back.

"That's my sister."

"I said, let's go," Melani demanded, taking the lead in the game of tug-of-war.

"You look familiar," Makai said, squinting his eyes while looking into Mahogany's face. "I know you from somewhere." Mahogany smiled at Makai and yanked her arm from her sister's grip. "Go upstairs, Melani," Mahogany urged. "I'll be there in a minute." With her forearm still in his grip, Makai led Mahogany away from the crowded entrance and over to the dozens of mailboxes lined on the lobby wall.

"I *should* look familiar to you," Mahogany said. "We used to see each other all the time in the window."

"Yes, that's it! The window," Makai said, smiling. "Our windows are so far away that it's hard to see ya face clearly. I'm glad I'm finally seeing you up close and in person because now I can see how beautiful you really are." Mahogany blushed, bowing her head from embarrassment.

"What's ya name?" Makai asked.

"Mahogany."

"That's a nice name."

"Mahogany, we need to get upstairs!" Melani called out, standing by the elevator. "And if you don't come right now, I *will* tell Mom."

"Yo, why is she trippin'?" Makai asked.

"We're supposed to go straight upstairs right after school."

"I'm sayin' though, can you come back downstairs in a little while? I wanna get to know you." A swarm of butterflies assaulted Mahogany's stomach. Anticipation, anxiety, and nerves twisted knots in Mahogany's gut.

"I can try."

"A'ight. I'll be right here." Mahogany looked over her shoulder as she approached the elevator. She turned just in time to catch Makai biting his lip seductively while his eyes were swerving up and around Mahogany's curvy hips. Mahogany smiled to herself and joined her sister in the elevator.

"What's the matter witchu?" Melani snapped.

"What?"

"Why were you standing there talking to that thug? You wanna get robbed or something?"

"He wasn't gonna rob me."

"Yeah, only because I was standing there and I kept calling you. If I would have gone upstairs like you said, those thugs probably would have surrounded you and tried to rape you or something."

"What?! Get outta here!"

"I'm serious. You don't know him. What you did was dangerous. Don't do that again."

Mahogany closed her eyes as the elevator door slammed shut. In her mind, just like in the lobby, Makai looked at her. Not just any look. He really *looked* at her, like Tafari used to *look* at her when they went out. The thought of that *look* chilled the back of her arms in the elevator. Mahogany needed to see him *look* at her again. But she had to figure out a way to shake free from Melani's prying eyes.

Chapter 6

Your women's worth is more than gold, clothes and material things/
You got the power to nourish seeds, and raise bastards into kings/

Those eyes. Mahogany's cheeks tingled under her face at the thought of *Makai's eyes* tracing her skin again. She stuck her face in front of the mirror to see what *those eyes* saw. Mahogany's lips curved from pleasure. *The bleaching cream is working already. You look lighter,* a voice in the back of her head said. *That's impossible*, another voice challenged. Mahogany ignored the negative voice and embraced the idea that the cream was working. Why else would Makai notice her? She had walked past boys in the halls before, and never did any one of them grab her like that.

Maybe it was the cornrows that twisted behind her head and down the middle of her back that made Makai notice her. Because of the cornrows and the cream, the air that dragged in and out of her nostrils was clearer; the blood in her veins seemed to flow smoother, carrying surges of energy that made it nearly impossible for her to sit still. Mahogany's teeth even appeared to be whiter. Maybe the teeth weren't whiter; she just never noticed them before. Never had a reason to show them until Karisma braided her hair and let her use the skin-bleaching cream.

Mahogany paced aimlessly in her room, trying to figure out a way to see *those eyes* again. She found herself in the kitchen, unsure of how she got there, opening the refrigerator door. *No milk.* Mahogany's eyes lit up when she realized there was nothing but orange juice on the top shelf. Suddenly, she had a taste for some cereal. "Melani, I'll be back!" Mahogany called out. "I'm going to the store!"

"Why are you going to the store?" Melani asked, rushing into the kitchen.

"We're outta milk."

"I can just call Mom and tell her to pick some milk up on her way home from work."

"I can't wait that long."

"Can't wait for what? Why do you need milk so bad?"

"I got a taste for some Apple Jacks," Mahogany answered, stepping into her sneakers.

"Since when do you eat Apple Jacks?"

"In about fifteen minutes when I come back."

"You trying to go see that boy, ain't you?"

"No, I'm not."

"Well, you shouldn't go out there by yourself. Lemme get my shoes and—"

"Don't bother. It'll only take me a few minutes. I'll be right back. Later!" Mahogany hurried through the front door and rushed into the staircase. Makai and his crew were still hanging by the entrance in the lobby. Mahogany stood by the bottom step and waited, hoping Makai would notice her. It didn't take long. He flashed his teeth and made his way toward her.

"Whassup, Mahogany?! I'm glad you made it back." Nerves only allowed Mahogany to smile but choked the words in her throat. She couldn't get them out. Makai took a seat on the second to last step and patted the slab of concrete to his left, inviting Mahogany to sit. Mahogany hugged her churning stomach to keep it from sinking while she sat beside him.

"So whassup witchu and me?" Makai asked, smile on his face. Mahogany's stomach sank lower and almost got away from her arms.

"What do you mean?" Mahogany asked, squeezing tighter.

"I want you to be bae."

"How am I gonna be bae, when you have a girl?"

"Girl? What girl?"

"I was looking out my window and I saw you with a girl the other night."

"Oh, her," Makai remembered, scratching the side of his head. "We broke up."

"Why?"

"Let's just say…it didn't work out."

"Why didn't it work out?"

"Because she wouldn't...You know what? Enough about her. I wanna talk about you."

"What about me?"

"I wanna talk about how good you look." Mahogany turned her head and *cheesed* at the cement wall. "I like ya braids, and you killin' dem jeans. No disrespect, but, stand up for me one more time so I can get another look atchu." Mahogany snickered into her cupped hands before covering her face completely as she slowly rose to her feet. She could feel Makai's eyes all over her. Mahogany plopped back down on the steps, still snickering into her hands.

"So you really like my braids?" Mahogany asked.

"I prefer long, straight hair, but your braids are fly too." Mahogany blushed at the comment. "So," Makai began, changing the subject. "You got a *bae* or what?"

"No, I'm not seeing anyone." Makai's black pearls gazed deep into her crescent eyes. They carefully traced the outline of Mahogany's oval face, pausing only to sample her thick, pouting lips. Mahogany was feeling hot from the inside out. Nearly melted into a puddle of hot chocolate on the steps.

"I feel like I gotta make my move quick before some other guy scoops you up." Mahogany faced the wall and *cheesed* again. Makai touched her hand, and an electric jolt circulated through her body. Her skin was alive; brought to life by the touch of his heavy hand, his fondling eyes, and his complimenting words.

One of Makai's boys wandered into the lobby and paused at the sight of Makai and Mahogany sitting side by side on the step. He smirked at Makai and nodded his head approvingly.

"Okay, playa!" One of the boys boasted with a sly smile. "You got another one, huh? I see you! I see you!"

"Yo, chill, Angel!" Makai shouted back through a nervous chuckle. "She ain't tryna hear all that."

Another boy with long dreadlocks entered the lobby. "Makai, de original Don Dada," the dreadlocked dude called out, voice seasoned with a heavy Jamaican accent.

"Can I get some privacy over here, y'all?" Makai pleaded.

"Ya want me to tell da boys dem fi gwan?" the dreadlocked dude asked.

"Nah, Zion, you don't have to tell them to go away. I'll leave." Makai turned to Mahogany. "Come on, let's bounce."

"Where are we going?"

"We can go to my apartment. No one's home, so we'll be alone and can talk without interruptions." Mahogany hesitated. She'd never been alone with a boy in his apartment before. Everything seemed to be moving so fast.

"I-I can't," Mahogany stammered.

"Why not?"

"Um, 'cause if my mom finds out I was at some boy's house, let's just say you won't wanna be me."

"How would she know?"

"My sister will tell her. Actually, I'm taking a big chance talking to you right now. I'm supposed to be at the store, and if I don't get back upstairs soon, my sister will be down here looking for me."

"You on punishment or something?"

"No, my mom don't like us to be outside when she ain't home."

"So, can you come back out when she gets home?"

"She won't let me because it'll be too dark when she gets home."

"So, let me get this straight. You're not supposed to come outside when ya moms ain't home and you can't come outside when she does get home because it'll be too dark. So, when do you come outside?"

"I don't." Mahogany shrugged. "Except when I go to my congregation meetings."

"Congregation meetings? What's that?"

"I'm a Jehovah's Witness."

"Jehovah's Witness?!" Makai bellowed. "Oh, hell naw! Not that! I'm wasting my time witchu!"

"Why you say that?"

"Jehovah Witness girls be on lockdown. Y'all can't do nothin'!"

"That's not true."

"Didn't you just finish tellin' me you can't come outside?" Mahogany fell silent. All of a sudden, Makai's face changed. The light in his eyes dimmed and his smirk melted away. He sported the same look he wore when he walked away from the girl who'd refused his advances the other night. Makai stood up and hovered over her.

His eyes drifted over to the lobby door. She figured it was just a matter of time before his legs followed his eyes. Mahogany's skin didn't want him to leave. She wanted his eyes to continue groping her and his heavy right palm to rub across the back of her hand. To keep him from walking away, Mahogany said, "We can always see each other in school."

"School? If we only see each other in school then we can't..." His eyes drifted back toward the door. He snapped, "Yo, lemme know somethin' right now so I don't waste my time. When I first saw you, I thought you were down. But if you gon' let ya mom dictate ya life and keep you on lockdown, then, I guess I was wrong about you. If you really wanna be wit' me, then you will make a way to see me. So let me know right now, you wanna be down wit' me or what?!" De-ja-vu chills raked up and down Mahogany's spine. The eerie scene felt like real life impersonating one of her window daydreams.

Before meeting Makai, when she would sit in her window, Mahogany filled her drawing pad with images of her and a random thug. She'd draw them on the corner, late, snuggling up under the nightlight of the moon. They would cuddle until day broke, right by the light pole. On special occasions, they'd gather with the rest of their unofficial family of thugs, spreading love like Thanksgiving; laughing, hugging, and enjoying each other's company.

Then they would disappear from the streets for days at a time doing God knows what. But it was finding out what only Makai and God knew that made her all the more curious. Mahogany's attraction to a thug like Makai was more than just the constant drama that lurked around the dark corners of his personality. It was the freedom he offered. Freedom from the arms of the suffocating relationship she was born into. The same arms that held her and her sister, tight, for all of their years. Arms that guided them into a monotonous life of weekly congregation meetings at the Kingdom Hall and locking themselves in their apartment after school until Mommy came home.

So there she sat. Just a few feet away from a guy who represented everything she thought she wanted. His words were an open-arm invitation to the streets. An embrace by the streets was a few words away from being realized. Words that Mahogany's fertile tongue was fully capable of bearing. Mahogany was just waiting for the right thug, any thug, to come along and plant the idea in her mind that he wanted to be with her. Makai was the right thug at the right time.

In an instant, Mahogany's mouth prematurely delivered the following words: "I'm down." Makai smiled and embraced the words like a newborn before cuddling Mahogany in his arms.

Makai pulled out his iPhone and said, "Lemme get ya number." After giving Makai her number, she cautioned, "I don't have my phone right now. My mom took it."

"What?" Makai asked, bowing his head in disgust.

"I got in trouble the other day, so my mom took my phone. Plus, she checks it all the time because I'm not allowed to receive calls from guys she doesn't know."

"You can program my number under a girl's name or something. How would she know?"

"What if she calls the number? Then what?"

"Then I'll play it off."

"I guess that can work. But like I said, my mom took my phone and I won't be getting it back for another week."

"We can communicate on Instagram or Snapchat."

"I don't have an Instagram or Snapchat account."

"Are you serious?" Makai asked, rhetorically. "So, what are we supposed to do now?"

"Well, I can give you my friend Karisma's number. You can call her and she can relay the messages to me."

"You cool wit' Karisma?" Makai asked with a hint of shock in his voice.

"Yeah. You sound surprised."

"I am."

"Why?"

"You and Karisma couldn't be any more different. Karisma is a wild girl; she *gets it in*."

"You ain't lying about that. Well, let me give you her number so—"

"I know how to get in touch wit' her," Makai cut her off.

"Well, I guess I better be going to the store so I can hurry back before my sister gets suspicious," Mahogany said, standing up. "Do you want to walk with me to the store?"

Slowly, a sinister smirk was chiseled into Makai's stone face. He said, "Nah. You go ahead. I'll catch up witchu later."

"Um, o-okay," Mahogany stammered, unsure of why he turned down her invitation. "So, I guess I'll see you at school tomorrow."

"Yeah," Makai answered quickly, turning and heading back to his crew in front of the building. Mahogany squeezed by the boys and headed to the store, unsure of how to feel. The commitment she gave to Makai on the staircase felt severed by the way he'd brushed her off. *Am I just overreacting?* Mahogany thought. Confusion clouded her thoughts as she walked down the block to the corner store. *Why the sudden change in his behavior? Did I do or say something wrong? Maybe I'm just overreacting. I'll just clear it all up with Makai when I get back from the store.*

When Mahogany returned from the store with a plastic bag of milk in hand, Makai and the boys were gone. Mahogany spent most of her anxious night gazing into Makai's bedroom window, watching for a light that would never come on. The rest of the night, Mahogany tossed and turned in her bed, dreaming that Makai had exited her life as quickly as he'd entered.

Chapter 7

You gotta keep ya head up and remain firm in your stance/ 'cause in this urban land/men degrade women who have a permanent tan/

As soon as Mahogany strode through the school doors the next morning, she met up with Karisma in the restroom on the first floor. She slid the straps of her backpack from her shoulders, kneeled down, and grabbed the tight jeans she stole from the mall the day before out of her bag. Karisma reached into her backpack and handed Mahogany a pair of black-on-white shell-toe Adidas and the shirt she stole for her. Mahogany stepped into one of the stalls, disrobed, shimmied her hips into the jeans, and pulled on the shirt. After slipping the sneakers on, Mahogany stepped out of the stall.

"Why didn't you just put your jeans on at home?" Karisma asked.

"My mother would kill me if she saw me in these fitted jeans," Mahogany announced, propping up on her tippy-toes to admire her butt in the mirror. "And thanks for the sneakers."

"Ya welcome. Are they too big?"

"A little. But it's okay. By the way, guess what happened to me on my way home yesterday?"

"What?" Karisma asked.

"I met a guy name Makai," Mahogany chirped.

"Yeah, I know."

"Know what?"

"About you and Makai."

"How do *you* know?"

"We face-timed last night."

"What for?"

"He wanted me to tell him all about you."

"Oh my God! What did you say?" Mahogany gasped, mouth gaping and hands clasped on each cheek.

"I told him you was mad-cool and pretty, and you was a good catch. But..."

"But what?"

"He said he thinks you might be too sheltered, and he's not sure if it's gonna work out between you and him."

"But last night, he asked me if I was willing to be *down with him*, and I said yes."

"He mentioned that," Karisma said, looking down and punching keys on her iPhone's keyboard. "But he said actions speak louder than words. So in other words, you can't just *tell him* you're down. You have to *show him* you're down." Before Mahogany could respond, the restroom door creaked open.

"Whassup, chica?!" a girl called out as she entered the restroom.

"About time you showed up, Ya Ya," Karisma said. "Ya Ya, this is Mahogany; Mahogany, this is my homegirl, Yahaira. But we call her Ya Ya." Ya Ya was a slim, curvy, golden-brown girl with long, black curly hair and freckles dotting the bridge of her nose and spread just under her almond-shaped eyes.

"Heeeyyy!" Mahogany greeted.

"Hola, chica!" Ya Ya said, extending her arms to give Mahogany a quick hug. "Oooohhh, I love ya braids, muy bonita. You look like an Egyptian queen."

"Thank you." Mahogany smiled. "Your hair is *muy bonita* too. Can I touch it?"

"Si, si." Ya Ya spun around, and Mahogany ran her fingers through her soft hair.

"I wish I had hair like yours," Mahogany said.

"You have no idea what I have to go through to get it to look like this," Ya Ya complained, her voice seasoned with a Spanish accent.

"At least it's yours."

"Those braids are yours too. You paid for them, no?"

"No, I paid for that hair, so technically it's mine," Karisma joked. The girls laughed.

"You mind if I ask you a question, Ya Ya?" Mahogany asked.

"Go 'head."

"You have a Spanish accent, yet, you don't look Spanish," Mahogany said, confusion wrinkling her face. "I'm confused because you look…black."

"I'm Dominican." Ya Ya smiled. "Most Dominicans have brown skin."

"So the difference between Dominicans and Puerto Ricans is Dominicans have darker skin?"

"Not necessarily. There are dark-brown-skinned Puerto Ricans too. The difference is Puerto Ricans are from Puerto Rico and Dominicans are either from the Dominican Republic or the Island of Dominica, which is where my mom is from. Oh yeah, Dominicans speak better Spanish." Ya Ya laughed.

"Y'all ready to roll or what?" Karisma asked.

"Ready to roll where?" Mahogany asked.

"To show and prove to Makai that you're down," Karisma said.

"Whatchu talking about?"

"Makai is having a hooky party at his apartment, and we're invited."

"Wait—what?" Mahogany asked.

"We're invited to a hooky party. You comin' or what?"

"I-I can't skip school two days in a row."

"Why not? You can do it, it's no big deal," Ya Ya chimed in, words seemingly jumping out of her mouth at one hundred miles per hour. "At the end of the day, it makes more sense to be absent two days in a row because it makes it seem like you were really sick."

"Yeah but—"

"Listen, Mahogany, I told Makai you were gonna be at the hooky party. What's he gonna think if you don't show up?" Mahogany was afraid to play hooky from school two days in a row, but she was more afraid of blowing her second shot at love. After being dumped by Tafari, Mahogany thought she had lost love forever, until she found it in the eyes of Makai while sitting on the project's steps. The love she thought she saw in Makai's eyes flickered and threatened to blow out like a worn-down candle when she mentioned that she was a Jehovah's Witness. *The hooky party*, Mahogany thought, *is a chance to rekindle the light in Makai's eyes.*

"Alright, let's go," Mahogany gave in. She reached into her backpack and removed the skin-bleaching cream that Karisma had given to her the day before.

"Whatchu doin'?" Karisma asked.

"Tryna look good for Makai," Mahogany said, smearing the cream all over her face.

"I told you that stuff don't work."

"Yes it does," Mahogany protested. "I think I see a difference already."

"You look the same to me, but whateva you say, girl," Karisma laughed. "Let's be out." Homeroom had just begun, so the halls were mostly empty of students. The coast was clear of the overzealous school resource officers, allowing the girls to snake around the corner and push through the back entrance and out into the streets.

Makai and four of his boys were already chillin' in front of the barbershop, which was across the street from Mahogany's building. Makai spotted Mahogany as they approached. In an instant, his eyes changed, and that *look* from the building lobby returned. That *look* chilled Mahogany's back.

"Glad you made it," Makai said, embracing Mahogany. "Wasn't sure if you were comin'."

"I told you I was down for you," Mahogany managed to say through an uneasy smile.

"No doubt. You kept ya word. I like that in a girl." Makai turned toward his boys and introduced Mahogany to them. "This is my boy, Angel; my boy over there with the red Yankee hat and fly gear is Jacario, aka Rio; my boy with the dreadlocks is Zion; and the big dude in the back is Donovan." Mahogany's heart fluttered at the sight of Donovan. That was the first time she laid eyes on him since the incident on the train when Donovan was accompanied by Dready and they had terrorized her and Tafari.

"You look familiar," Donovan said to Mahogany. "I know you from somewhere."

"Maybe we're in the same gym class or something," Mahogany lied, bowing her head and inching beside Makai.

At that moment, Karisma cuddled up beside Angel, running her fingers through his curly hair while Ya Ya playfully fought off Rio's advances. The scene was like a page out of Mahogany's drawing pad come to life.

About a week ago, Mahogany created a sketch while sitting in her window, watching the late-night *corner cinema*. The sketch detailed three thugs posted up against the brick wall of the barbershop in their thug poses, each with their arms wrapped around the lower waist of the girl cuddled up next to them.

The sketch had come alive right before Mahogany's two eyes as if someone hit the play button and the still movie on paper was no longer *still*. Mahogany never found out what happened next because she never sketched a follow-up. But like an improv actress, Mahogany had to act on impulse. Depending on her next move, it could result in her continuing her new career with Makai, or she'd literally be back to the drawing board behind her bedroom window.

"Come on, y'all, let's go upstairs," Makai urged. Mahogany braced herself. She remembered sitting in her window watching girls and thugs, hand in hand, walking off the block and disappearing to God knows where. Mahogany was about to find out what God knew.

Upon entering Makai's living room, Mahogany sank into a seat on the mustard-colored couch and pinned herself against the arm of the couch. Karisma and Angel snuggled up on the love seat, Ya Ya and Rio were huddled over the stove making Ramen Noodles, and Zion and Donovan were sitting at the kitchen table opening up Sprite bottles.

"Yo Angel, I thought Sleep was comin' through to chill wit' us?" Makai asked.

"Nah, he couldn't make it. He's in school, makin' that money."

"Facts."

"Me and Rio is missing out on a lot of bread by being here," Angel revealed. "We need to get this party started now so me and Rio can sneak into school during lunchtime and make up on all the money we are missing out on." *How are they missing out on money by not being in school?* Mahogany asked herself. *Are there special classes in school that pay students money that I don't know anything about? I'm so confused.*

"Yo, Don!" Rio called out, turning from the stove. "I heard you got punked by some li'l dude from the Northside the other day. Heard he took ya girl's chain while you stood there like a lame and you ain't do nothin' 'bout it."

"Who told you that?!" Donovan grunted, turning around in his seat.

"It's all over the school, man. Everybody talkin' 'bout it."

"Everybody needs to shut up!" Donovan grunted again. "Won't none of them say it to my face."

"What's the kid's name that took ya girl's chain?" Makai asked, taking a seat beside Mahogany.

"My homegirl Kesha told me it was some dude named Tafari," Rio cut in. Mahogany's eyes widened but her mouth remained closed.

"Dat's de ras-clot bwoy dat lick off a shot in me brother Dready's leg," Zion snarled. "As soon me brother heal up, de yankee bwoy will pay!"

"Yo, Don. You gonna let that kid get away with punkin' you in front of ya girl like that?" Rio asked, sarcastic smirk wrinkling his lips.

"Yo, Rio, man, you need to mind ya business!" Donovan seethed. "The only reason he got the chain was because he had his boys with him. Don't worry, it ain't over." Zion walked over to Makai and handed him a bottle of Sprite.

"You wanna sip?" Makai asked, eagerly shoving the plastic bottle to Mahogany's lips.

"No thank you. I'm not thirsty," Mahogany answered, pulling away.

"Come on, just one little sip, for me."

"Okay." Mahogany gave in and took a sip. "Yuck!" She gagged, jumping back from the bottle. "What kind of Sprite is that?"

"It's lean, my gal," Zion chimed in.

"Lean?"

"My insides are on fire," Mahogany revealed. Everyone laughed.

Over the next hour, the crew ate chicken-flavored Ramen Noodles, sipped lean—except for Mahogany—and watched music videos. Donovan remained seated at the kitchen table, by himself, seething in his own thoughts.

Mahogany glanced at the DVD player to the right of the flat-screen television to check the time. It was nine thirty in the morning. She should have been in biology class working with her lab partner, Imani Lewis. Instead, Mahogany was in a foreign apartment with a new lab partner. The twinkle in Makai's eyes warned that he was ready to experiment.

The touch of his fingers on the back of Mahogany's hand sent waves of shivers up and down her left arm. Makai hooked his arm around Mahogany's neck and reeled her face into his. "Can I taste them luscious lips?" Makai asked, his face inches from Mahogany's.

"N-Not now," Mahogany stammered, pulling away.

"What's the matter?" Makai asked.

"Nothing, umm—"

"I know what it is. It's too many eyes in here. It's making you nervous, huh? Let's go to my room where we'll have some privacy." Mahogany wanted to say no and refuse his advances, but she was brought back to her window, when she'd watched Makai try to force his lips on that girl a couple of nights ago. She'd refused his advances and turned her face away from him. Soon after, Makai turned away from *her* and never looked back.

But unlike *that light-skinned girl*, Mahogany didn't have any other prospects. While Mahogany sat on Makai's couch, contemplating whether to go with him to his bedroom, Mahogany figured that light-skinned girl was probably snuggling up to the right or left of some thug on his couch. Mahogany was sure that the moment Makai dumped that other girl, dozens of other couch seat cushions were immediately available for her next to guys from school who were impatiently waiting for her to become single. If Makai turned away from Mahogany, the only couch seat cushion that would be available to her would be the one she had been leaving butt imprints and farting on since she was five: her mother's red suede love seat.

Makai jumped up and grabbed Mahogany by the hand. Reluctantly and slowly, she allowed him to lead her into his bedroom.

"Where ya goin', my yute?" Zion asked. "Me 'bout to spark up de ganja!"

"I don't want any," Makai called back. "I'm 'bout to spark up Mahogany!"

"Yes, Don Dada!" Zion cheered.

After closing the door, Makai cut off all the lights in his room and sealed the blinds shut. His brown skin tone was superbly camouflaged behind the shadows in his obscure room. Mahogany froze at the door. Only the whites of Makai's eyes were visible as he sat on the edge of his twin-size bed. He patted the seat beside him, urging Mahogany to sit.

Mahogany heard her mother's voice in the back of her mind, *remember your morals*. But it was something about Makai's smile, his rep, and his eyes that choked the good sense out of her. Mahogany cautiously made her way over to the bed and sank in a seat beside Makai. His face inched toward hers. His face hovered so close to Mahogany's, she could feel the heat from his nose blowing on her mouth like a blow dryer. His dark stare gazed into her eyes, seeming to say, *you ready?* If being at a hooky party and being alone with Makai in his room was sticking her toe in the water, what was about to go down was like submerging her entire body below the surface. And that's how she felt; fully submerged. She felt trapped. Couldn't breathe. Anxiety surging through her body. Her heart pounding like a jackhammer. She was drowning.

"I-I have to go to the bathroom," Mahogany announced, squirming around Makai. Mahogany raced from the bedroom and darted into the bathroom. Mahogany's thoughts, like her breathing, were scattered. She couldn't catch her breath nor hold a thought in place. But the one thought that ran the wildest in her brain was whether or not to lock herself in the bathroom and never come out. Her mom's words circulated in her mind again. A sense of guilt overwhelmed her. A part of Mahogany wanted to run from the guilt, but the rest of her wanted to soak in it. Tears scattered down her face as she paced in circles. She flushed the toilet to give the impression that she was actually *using* the bathroom.

"What am I doing? What am I doing?" Mahogany mumbled to herself, wiping tears with the back of her hand.

"You a'ight in there?" Makai barked, banging on the door.

"Yeah. Be out in a minute!" Mahogany called back.

"You been in there for over ten minutes!" Makai called back.

Ten minutes? It's been that long? Mahogany paused in the middle of her pace to catch a glimpse of the girl in the mirror. The glimpse turned into a long stare. "What have you gotten yaself into?" Mahogany asked the girl in the mirror.

This is what you wanted, right? her reflection seemed to answer back.

"Not exactly," Mahogany said. "I asked for someone to love me. I didn't ask for…for…"

Sex! Go 'head and say it. Don't be shy now!

"Sex. There, I said it."

Listen, it's all a part of the package. When you mess with a thug, it's all about alcohol, drugs, sex, and violence. And you knew that, too. You smelled the weed on his clothes the first day you met him. Your sister pulled you away, but you escaped and ran back to him. After he found out what you're really about, he was about to turn his back on you, but still you cut school and ran back to him. So, either open that door and claim Makai, or remain locked in here, all alone without a man, like you will be for the rest of your life.

Mahogany's trembling hand reached for the door handle. She clutched it, but fear and anxiety paralyzed her hand. "I can't open it," Mahogany cried to her reflection. Her reflection didn't respond. Mahogany was all alone.

"Mahogany! You comin' out or what?" Makai called out from the other side of the door.

"Yo, Mo, you okay?" Karisma banged on the door. "You been in there for over fifteen minutes!"

"It's de lean, mon! It's de lean! She can't take it; she sick!" Zion called out. Mahogany's head was throbbing as if the fists that were pounding on the door were actually pounding on her forehead. Before long, every loud voice on the other side of the bathroom door blended together until it was one incoherent ball of noise. She took a seat on the side of the tub and wept into her hands.

Chapter 8

Kinky hair and full lips may seem like an odd privilege/
But when you look in the mirror you're seeing the reflection of God's image/

With the extension braids out of Mahogany's hair and the skin-bleaching cream jar empty, her face was exposed. Her face was naked. Mahogany's natural hair was now pulled back into a ponytail and her face was out in the open. The slight confidence that had weaved its way onto Mahogany's face when Karisma braided the extensions into her hair three weeks ago was now tangled in the discarded extension braids bunched in a plastic shopping bag on Karisma's bedroom floor. The empty jar of the skin-bleaching cream was also in the shopping bag. Mahogany's face felt dry and unloved. She glared in disgust at the girl in the mirror. The no-confidence-havin', no guy-gettin' lame girl was back. The longer she stared, the more convinced Mahogany became that the girl in front of her eyes couldn't compete with the girl behind her eyes; the light-skinned girl with the long weave that had been on Mahogany's mind all week ever since she saw her walking through the halls of Hard Knocks all boo'd up with Makai. The thought of Makai had Mahogany fighting back tears.

"You a'ight, Mahogany?" Karisma asked, sitting on the edge of her bed.

"I can't stop thinking about him," Mahogany whined, eyes watering up again. "Ever since the hooky party almost three weeks ago, he's all I've been thinking about. He hasn't answered any of my calls or responded to my texts. When I see him in the halls, he acts like he doesn't even know me. I haven't been eating, I can barely sleep; I can't concentrate in class. I miss him so much."

"Well, chica, at the end of the day, you kind of did it to yaself," Ya Ya chimed in. "That hooky party was about to be lit until you locked yaself in that bathroom for a half hour and killed the whole vibe of our party."

"Come on, Ya Ya," Karisma laughed. "Why you gon' bring that up again? We done clowned Mahogany to death over what happened at the hooky party."

"It's all good. I deserve it," Mahogany acknowledged. "Karisma, can you do my hair for me?"

"Didn't we skip school today so I could take the old braids out and redo it?"

"I never said I wanted you to put in more braids."

"So, what do you want me to do?"

"Can you make my hair look like that girl we saw walking with Makai in the cafeteria last week?"

"You talkin' 'bout that light-skinned girl with the buck teeth?"

"Yeah."

"That girl had a Brazilian hair weave."

"Can you do it for me?"

"Girl, stop playing," Karisma chuckled.

"I'm serious."

"I'm serious too. I can braid hair all day, but I don't know how to do no full head weave."

"I think you should stick with braids," Ya Ya cut in. "You look good with braids. They really fit the shape of ya face."

"Thanks, Ya Ya. But guys don't care about no braids. They want their girls to have long hair."

"So, you really think just by gettin' a hair weave, you gonna get Makai back?" Ya Ya asked.

"I don't know." Mahogany shrugged. "Even though he liked my braids, he told me that he prefers long hair."

"Girl, let me tell you something." Karisma stood up, serious look on her face. "In order for us dark-skinned girls to keep a dude like Makai, we gotta do what them light-skinned girls won't do, ya feel me?" Mahogany blushed. Karisma continued, "I'm just keeping it real witchu. When you get invited to a hooky party, you can't front and then lock yaself in the bathroom and think you're gonna get a second chance. If you were one of them light-skinned goddesses that the guys all worship, then you would get a second, third, and however many chances it took for them to get witchu. But not us." Karisma paused and stuffed her right hand into her pocket. "You wanna get Makai back?"

Mahogany nodded.

"And you wanna keep him?"

"You know I do." Karisma removed her hand from her pocket, grabbed Mahogany's left wrist, and placed something that felt like plastic into her hand. Fear, confusion, and embarrassment lit up in Mahogany's widened eyes when she looked down into her hand. She threw it on the floor and jumped back as if the item Karisma gave to her had come alive in her hand. "What am I supposed to do with that?" Mahogany asked.

"If you don't know what to do with a condom, then you can forget about gettin' back with Makai," Karisma laughed.

"I mean, I know what it's for...it's just that—"

"Do you want your man back or do you wanna be miserable?" Karisma interrupted, kneeling down to snatch the condom from the floor before stuffing it back into Mahogany's hand. "Do what you gotta do or watch someone like Malikah take him from you."

"Malikah? You know her?" Mahogany asked.

"Not personally. I mean, I never talked to her or anything like that, but I still can't stand her. You can tell she thinks she's all that."

"Tell me about it," Mahogany chimed in. "Me and her got into a fight."

"Get outta here. When?"

"Almost a month ago in the pizza shop. Actually, it was more of a pushing-and-shoving match. She's the one that cracked the 'you so black' joke on me. She's the reason why Nevaeh and Nyla called me Soy Sauce."

"You still got beef with Malikah?"

"Yeah, she threatened me, talkin' 'bout she gonna see me again. We haven't crossed paths since that day though."

"Remember what I told you when we first met? An enemy of my friend is…wait, I mean—"

"You mean *the enemy of my enemy is my friend*." Mahogany laughed.

"Yeah, that's it! That's the quote, exactly!"

"I googled it after you tried to say it to me in the restroom."

"Anyway, I've been looking for a reason to put hands on Malikah. Now I got one. As a matter of fact, the next light-skinned chick I see, they gettin' beat up on sight!"

"Karisma, lemme ask you something?" Ya Ya asked, changing the subject. She'd had a quizzical look on her face ever since Karisma was rattling on about dark-skinned girls.

"Go 'head."

"You said that guys prefer light-skinned girls over dark-skinned girls, right?"

"Yeah."

"But that's not true. My skin is brown, and I got mad-dudes tryna get wit' me."

"You're different, Ya Ya."

"How?"

"First of all, you're brown, but not as brown as me and Mahogany. Second, you're Dominican, and dudes love y'all Dominican and Puerto Rican girls wit y'all Spanish accents. And third, you got long hair all down your back. Seriously, Ya Ya, you my girl and e'erything, but you can't relate to what me and Mahogany go through on a daily basis."

"But I *can* relate. I may not know what it's like to be a dark-skinned black girl. But I know what it's like to be a dark-skinned Dominican girl. And being the darkest one in my family ain't easy. My family don't even call me by my name. They call me morena."

"What does morena mean?" Mahogany asked.

"It means dark skin," Ya Ya answered before continuing. "When they would call me morena when I was younger, it was cute, I guess. But as I got older and realized that my skin was darker than everyone else's in my family, the nickname started to bother me. So, I just wanted to let y'all know that African-Americans ain't the only ones that have to deal with having darker skin."

"Wow, that's deep, Ya Ya," Mahogany said. "I never knew other ethnicities dealt with dark-skin issues."

"Yeah, it's deep," Karisma interjected. "But I'll take your problems over mine any day of the week. And your hair too." Karisma and Mahogany laughed.

"Don't act like you ain't used to have long hair," Ya Ya remarked, snatching a picture from Karisma's dresser and handing it to Mahogany.

"Wow, your hair is really long in this picture, Karisma," Mahogany mentioned. "How old were you?"

"I was like seven years old in that picture."

"Why do you always keep it hidden under that scarf?"

"My hair don't look like that anymore."

"What happened?"

"My mom got tired of dealing with my hair because it was so thick and long," Karisma admitted. "So she decided to give me a kiddie perm. She really didn't know what she was doing. Over the years my hair started thinning out and breaking off. Then, she got sick of it and started taking me to the African braiders on Gun Hill Road. They would braid my hair so tight, it would cause too much tension in my hair. That's why my edges are so jacked up now. What I learned over the years is, the less you do to your hair, the better."

"Wow, that's messed up," Ya Ya said.

"Tell me about it," Karisma added, shaking her head.

"Speaking of hair, how much is it gonna cost if I go to a beauty parlor?" Mahogany asked Karisma.

"Did you hear what I just said? Less is more."

"Since when did guys prefer girls with less hair? According to guys, more is always better than less—"

"That's not what I meant—"

"Are you gonna tell me how much its gonna cost or what?"

"Probably about two hundred dollars."

"Dag!"

"Yeah, it's expensive."

"I have about one hundred and fifty dollars saved up from my allowance. I was gonna use it to buy some more clothes and another jar of the skin-bleaching cream. I think I'm going to use it to get my hair done. I just need to figure out how I'm gonna get the rest."

"Don't waste ya money on that cream," Karisma warned. "I been tryna tell you, I tried it and it didn't work. All the cream is supposed to do is even out your skin tone if you got dark spots. You don't have any dark spots on your face. Your skin ain't uneven. It's not supposed to turn you into a light-skinned girl."

"I think you're wrong," Mahogany said, shaking her head. "I've been putting that cream on for a couple of weeks, and I think my face did get a little lighter." Mahogany examined her face in the mirror one more time.

"Your face looks exactly the same to me as when I first metchu." Ya Ya shrugged. "It's just as brown and just as beautiful."

"So why don't I feel beautiful?"

"Oh, before I forget," Ya Ya began, changing the subject and reaching into her backpack. "Here are the two Polo shirts I promised you."

"Thanks, Ya Ya!" Mahogany cheered, draping the red one over her torso and looking at herself in the mirror. "Are you sure you want to give these Polos away?"

"Girl please, I got a closet full of Polos. Rio keeps me laced."

The girls spent the next few hours watching Netflix and raiding Karisma's refrigerator.

How could I get my hands on fifty dollars? was the question that held Mahogany's mind hostage when she exited Karisma's apartment, when she met up with Melani at school, and when she arrived home. Her mind was so occupied with finding realistic answers to her question, she ignored Melani's barrage of questions as they walked home.

Mahogany made a beeline straight for her bedroom with Melani trailing closely behind. "I still wanna know how you managed to take ya braids out in school? It's impossible to take them out while you're in class unless—"

"Watch ya face," Mahogany warned, slamming her bedroom door behind her. Mahogany opened her dresser drawer and removed an envelope that secured her one hundred and fifty dollars. "*Fifty more*," she mumbled to herself. With the dresser drawer still open, Mahogany noticed several coins scattered under loose socks. The coins gave her an answer to the question. Not the best answer, but an answer.

An old fish bowl sat in the middle of her dresser, full to the brim with an assortment of bronze and silver coins. Her hand plunged into the bowl and fished up a fistful of pennies, quarters, dimes, and nickels. She tossed the useless bronze coins back into the bowl like small fish and spread the silver ones across her bed. Over the next ten minutes, Mahogany's hand took continuous dips into the pool of change in the fish bowl until all that was left were dull pennies, sunken at the bottom. Mahogany counted up the silver coins and was fifteen dollars closer to her goal. "Only thirty-five dollars to go," Mahogany sighed. "Where am I gonna get it from?"

An answer that had been offered as soon as the question first developed, but was rejected almost immediately by her conscience, re-entered her thoughts. The voice of her conscience was quieted by the loud thoughts of possibly reuniting with Makai. Memories of her crying after witnessing Makai walking the halls of Hard Knocks with other girls and more memories of her many sleepless nights crowded into her brain. Her head was a stadium of noise, all cheering her on and urging her to accept the answer. Her conscience, now a mere whisper, drowned in the chants. The chants pushed her forward.

Mahogany inched her bedroom door open, crept across the hall, and snuck into her mother's bedroom. The girls weren't allowed in their mother's bedroom when she wasn't home, so Mahogany had to be extra quiet because eavesdropping-Melani was in the living room doing homework or something.

Carefully, Mahogany closed her mother's bedroom door behind her. She tiptoed to her mother's nightstand and opened the bottom drawer. Mahogany eyed the brown King James Bible, closed her eyes, and hesitated to touch it. The voice of her conscience grew louder than a whisper, and for a moment, through the noise in her head, Mahogany heard, *Don't do it! It's not right*! Just as quickly, the voice of her conscience was overwhelmed by chants: *Do it for*

Makai! Do it for love! No more sleepless nights! Mahogany inhaled, and removed the Bible.

An unsealed, thick envelop stuck out of the top and bottom of the Bible like a giant bookmark. Mahogany opened the Bible and removed the envelope. *In case of emergency* was inscribed on it. Just as she removed the envelope, her eyes ran across the words: Leviticus 19:11. She quickly closed the Bible before her eyes could read the chapter and verse.

As Mahogany opened the envelope and removed the thick stack of greenbacks, she felt a twinge in her stomach. Mahogany knew it was her conscience trying a different way to communicate with her. She ignored it and counted the money. "Wow, five hundred and twenty dollars," Mahogany said to herself in amazement. Even though she only needed thirty-five dollars, Mahogany removed sixty, just in case Karisma's math was off and the cost of getting her hair done was more than both of them originally thought. Her conscience, not going down without a fight, twisted knots in her gut as Mahogany slipped the sixty dollars in her pocket. Mahogany reasoned with herself that she would replace the money once she got her allowance from her mom. Unfortunately, it would take about four allowances, so the money wouldn't be replaced for weeks.

Mahogany shoved the envelope back in the Bible, placed it back in the drawer, closed it, and headed for the door. When she closed her mother's bedroom door behind her, something flashed across her vision like a spirit.

Mahogany's head snapped up. Melani was standing at the end of the hall. The sisters stared at each other like two Wild West gunslingers at high noon in some deserted ghost town. Instead of long barrel Colt 45s, they were shooting dirty looks at each other. Glaring into each other's eyes, it was almost as if they could read each other's thoughts.

Telepathically, Mahogany could have sworn she heard Melani say, *What were you doing in Mommy's room?* Mahogany peered into Melani's beady eyes and screamed in her head, *None of ya business*! Mahogany was sure Melani heard that thought because she twisted her lips and frowned. Mahogany headed into her bedroom, calling a truce for the moment.

Before her body completely disappeared into her room, Mahogany shot her one last glare and, in her head, warned, *If you snitch, we'll meet again, same time, same place. And instead of dirty looks, fists will be flying*! She didn't know if her sister heard that one, but for her own good and Mahogany's, she hoped so.

Chapter 9

Motherland blood running through ya veins below the surface/
Of ya African skin which is the same color as the Earth is/

"I got the money to get my hair done," Mahogany cheered, walking side by side with Karisma through the halls of Bronx High. "I made an appointment for tomorrow."

"Yesterday you were saying you didn't have enough. Where did you get the rest of the money so fast?" Karisma asked.

"My mom."

"She gave it to you?"

"No, I borrowed it."

"You mean, you stole it!"

"I'm gonna pay her back."

"I taught you well, huh?" Karisma chuckled. The halls were overflowing with students changing classes. Karisma paused and nudged Mahogany with her elbow. "Look, there goes ya homegirl Malikah," Karisma joked.

"That ain't my homegirl," Mahogany snapped. "Where is she?"

"Right there," Karisma pointed. Mahogany strained her neck and spotted Malikah's face amongst the crowd of students walking toward them.

"Watch this. I'mma bump her when she walks by," Karisma said. As Malikah approached, Karisma stuck out her shoulder and slammed it against Malikah's, causing her to drop her books.

"Damn! Watch where you going!" Malikah barked, kneeling down to retrieve her books.

"Who you think you talkin' to!" Karisma barked, hovering over her. Malikah's face was twisted with anger until she stood up and realized that Karisma was taller and bigger than she was. Malikah chomped down on her bottom lip, biting off the response.

"That's what I thought!" Karisma shouted as Malikah hurried down the hall.

"Them ugly dark-skinned chicks always hatin' on me," Malikah said, loud enough for Mahogany and Karisma to hear.

"What did you say!" Karisma bellowed. She chased after Malikah and was about to attack her from behind until Mr. Garrison stepped outside of his classroom. Karisma froze in her tracks and watched Malikah enter Mr. Garrison's classroom. "This ain't over!" Karisma warned.

***

Mahogany had just arrived home from school when her cell phone rang. She glanced at the screen and saw that it was Karisma.

"Hey Karisma."

"Meet me by the elevator!"

"Why?"

"Don't ask questions! Just hurry up!"

"Um…all right," Mahogany replied. She knew Melani would ask her where she was going, so she grabbed the half-full garbage from the kitchen and headed to the door.

"Where ya going?" asked Melani, who was sitting in the living room doing homework.

"To the incinerator," Mahogany responded and hurried through the door. After stuffing the garbage bag in the incinerator, Mahogany saw Karisma rounding the corner. Karisma's face was masked with the same scowl she wore six hours earlier, the moment after Malikah dissed her in the school hallway. The person behind her eyes looked different, though. Different from the usual agitated girl who stalked behind her eyes. The new person taking up residence behind her glassy black-pearl eyes was hard for Mahogany to read. And it made her uneasy. It made her stay on guard.

"I need you to come with me across the street," Karisma demanded.

"For what?"

"I need to handle something right quick."

"But I—"

"It's for both of us. Come on!" The elevator door dragged open, and the girls squeezed between the bodies that packed the crammed space. Mahogany couldn't keep her eyes off of Karisma's. It appeared as though Karisma was staring through Mahogany, looking at something that only she could see. And whatever it was, it seemed to slowly agitate her. Karisma's stone face started to crumble. Water gathered in her dark eyes, then slowly dribbled down her cheeks, molding and shaping the scowl into something more menacing.

By the time the elevator reached the first floor, Mahogany didn't even recognize the deranged-looking Karisma anymore.

"Walk with me over here right quick," the stranger that looked like Karisma ordered. Mahogany followed her until they stopped at the corner, directly across the street from Jackie's Caribbean Kitchen. Karisma paused behind a blue mailbox.

Karisma leaned forward on it, folded her arms on top, and stood as still as a sniper. Her eyes, like a scope on top of a rifle, remained steady on the door of Jackie's. And they didn't budge, despite the fury of cars racing back and forth in the street in front of her vision. Despite the many students, especially them light-skinned boys that Karisma loved so much, who strutted back and forth past the door. And despite the slight drizzle of rain that beat on the scarf that covered her hair.

Mahogany removed her hands from her pocket and flipped the hood over her head. Karisma's hands didn't move. Neither did her hood. Or her eyes. They remained on the door while it swung open and closed as people spilled out, clutching plastic bags that held containers of Jamaican food.

Suddenly, Karisma's eyes flickered. Then they moved. And her body followed. She stepped into the street, her feet dancing in place. Karisma's jittery eyes went from the door, to the traffic in the street, and back to the door. Mahogany's eyes beat Karisma across the street. She saw a line of unfamiliar faces exiting Jackie's. The people gathered in front of the entrance until, one by one, they broke apart and went their separate ways down the street. Left standing at the entrance was Malikah and some dude. They hugged, and the dude quickly made his way down the sidewalk and disappeared around the corner. Malikah walked to the curb and just stood there.

No longer dancing in place, Karisma was dancing in between moving cars, hurrying toward Malikah. Mahogany danced the same dance as Karisma, trying to avoid the moving cars as she made her way across the street.

Just as Karisma's tan Timberland boot hit the sidewalk, she reached into her mouth and pulled out a small razor. Seemingly out of nowhere, a platinum Acura screeched to a halt right in front of the curb Malikah was standing at. A dude jumped out, opened the passenger door, and Malikah slid into the seat. She had no idea how close her face was to being carved up like a Halloween pumpkin. The dude raced back to the driver's side, jumped in, and the car sped off. At that point, Mahogany had caught up to Karisma. She saw the razor being held between the tip of her thumb and index finger. Mahogany wondered, how was Karisma able to talk with the razor blade in her mouth that whole time?

"She's so lucky," Karisma mumbled, sinister tone in her voice. "I was about to carve all that light skin off her face!" Mahogany knew all too well how Malikah's comments could affect a person. "This ain't over," Karisma said under her breath before walking up the block and disappearing between the buildings.

Chapter 10

Queens fightin' queens? Ya lost ya mind, ya self-respect and ya crown/
Instead of lifting each other up, sisters are beating each other down/

"Oh my God! Ya hair looks so good!" Karisma cheered as they walked to the cafeteria.

"Thanks, girl," Mahogany said, beaming from ear to ear.

"Turn around!" Karisma demanded. Mahogany twisted her neck so the girls could see the back of her new hair.

"I love it," Ya Ya added, moving closer to examine Mahogany's hair. "Muy bonita!"

"Yo, whatcha mom say about ya hair?" Karisma asked. "I know she was trippin' when she saw it."

"She ain't see it yet. By the time she got home last night, my hair was wrapped and tied up in my scarf."

"I should take a picture of you," Karisma suggested, removing her iPhone from her back pocket and positioning it in front of Mahogany. "Say Brazilian!"

"Brazilian!" Mahogany laughed.

"I'mma post this on my Instagram page," Karisma claimed.

The girls chatted and laughed with each other as they entered the cafeteria and joined the long lunch line.

"You already got twenty likes!"

"Fareal?" Mahogany beamed.

"Wait a minute. I just got three direct messages," Karisma announced. "The first one is from Jalen and it says, 'Who is ya friend and does she have a boyfriend?'"

"Which Jalen? Tall Jalen?" Ya Ya asked.

"No, fat Jalen."

"Ewwww!"

"Lemme see him," Mahogany demanded, leaning in to get a better look at Karisma's iPhone.

"He's ugly, ain't he?" Ya Ya laughed.

"I wouldn't say he's ugly, but—"

"But you wouldn't want to be his girlfriend, trust me!" Ya Ya and Mahogany shared a look before laughing together.

"Who are the other two messages from?" Mahogany asked.

"Amir and—"

"Amir? I don't know him either. Can I see?" Karisma held her iPhone before Mahogany's eyes. "He's kinda cute."

"He said the same thing about you in the message Amir sent."

"Fareal."

"Guess who the last message is from?"

"Who?"

"Makai! He said, 'Is that Mahogany?'"

"Makai?!"

"Yeah, and I just responded to him."

"What did you say?"

"I said, 'Yes. Ain't she beautiful?'"

"Did he respond yet?" Mahogany asked, energy in her voice and body.

"Yeah, just now."

"Lemme see!" Mahogany nearly climbed up Karisma's back, trying to peek over her shoulder to see Makai's response.

"Yo, chill!" Karisma complained. "You almost made me drop my phone!"

"My bad. I just wanna see what he said."

"He said you 'look real good.' And he wants to see you."

"Oh my God! What should I say?"

"Don't worry about it," Karisma said, typing a response. "I'm sayin' it for you."

"Wait, Karisma!" Mahogany shrieked, grabbing Karisma's arm. "What are you typing?"

"I said you will meet him before school tomorrow. And he said he can't wait."

"What!" Mahogany gasped. "Meet him before school? Does that mean he's expecting me to cut school again?"

"Yup. And now you are getting a second chance. Ain't that whatchu wanted?"

"Yeah, but—"

"Look, you got a second chance. Don't blow it this time." Mahogany was excited, concerned, and worried all at the same time. Excited to get a second chance with Makai, concerned about skipping school again, and worried about getting caught by her mom. While Mahogany stewed in her thoughts, Karisma and Ya Ya joked and laughed with each other.

"I'm thinking about gettin' my hair done like Mahogany's," Karisma revealed.

"Say *word*," Ya Ya laughed. "You gon' finally take off that scarf?"

"Fa sho," Karisma said. "You see how fast Mahogany got Makai back after gettin' her hair did?"

"Yeah, not to mention twenty likes on Instagram in like twenty minutes."

"Make that thirty likes in twenty-five minutes," Karisma said, checking her Instagram page on her phone. "Do you think I would look good if I got my hair done like Mahogany's?" Before Ya Ya could respond, two girls standing in line directly behind them started laughing.

"Yo, who y'all laughin' at! Huh?" Karisma snapped. Mahogany turned around and recognized the two girls: Zuri, who was in her art class, and Imani, her lab partner in science. Zuri and Imani were startled, and they took a backwards step as Karisma approached them. "Y'all laughin' at me?"

"What are you talking about?" Zuri asked.

"Y'all were laughin' at me. I saw y'all."

"My sista, I promise you, we were not laughing at you. We were laughing at—"

"Who you calling sista?"

"You. We're all sistas."

"I ain'tcha damn sista!" Karisma huffed, inching closer to Zuri.

"Sista, please get out of my face."

"Whatchu gon' do about it!"

"Karisma, chill!" Mahogany pleaded, grabbing a handful of Karisma's arm and trying to pull her away from Zuri.

"Nah, I ain't gon' chill!" Karisma snapped, yanking her arm from Mahogany's grip. "These high yellow chicks be thinkin' they all that, that's why I can't stand 'em." Karisma extended her finger and put it on Zuri's forehead. "Laugh at me again and see what happens!"

"Get ya finger outta my face!" Zuri barked, knocking Karisma's finger from her forehead. Karisma reached down, grabbed a Styrofoam tray from the rack, and in one motion swung and slapped Zuri across the face. Before Zuri could react, Karisma already had two handfuls of Zuri's hair, and she yanked her to the ground before falling on top of her. Both girls were rolling around on the cafeteria floor, yelling, tugging, and scratching. Students were dropping their lunch trays, climbing over lunch tables, and pushing and shoving each other out of the way to get a front-row look at the fight. Mahogany spotted two resource officers bursting through the band of students, closing in on the two combatants. Quickly, Mahogany and Imani reached down and grabbed each combatant by their shoulders, trying to pull them apart before the resource officers reached them. They were too late.

The resource officers swooped down and untangled Zuri and Karisma. Mahogany felt a strong hand wrap around her forearm like a vise. She turned and realized the hand belonged to Mr. Sullivan, the school's vice principal. Karisma, Zuri, and Imani were being led through the cafeteria entrance by the resource officers, and Mahogany was being pulled in the same direction. "Where are you taking me? I didn't do anything!" Mahogany pleaded.

"You were fighting. I saw you," Mr. Sullivan replied, rushing Mahogany through the cafeteria entrance and into the hall. They were right behind the resource officers, Karisma, Zuri, and Imani.

"I wasn't fighting. I was trying to break it up!" Mr. Sullivan ignored her pleas and ushered her into the front office with the other girls.

***

Mahogany eased into the passenger seat of her mother's black Altima. The seat was about as comfortable as a mound of rocks. Mom didn't say a word in the principal's office. Didn't even look in Mahogany's direction. She sat, stone faced, as Vice Principal Sullivan spoke about the fight and the consequences.

"Ma, I promise you, I was not fighting," Mahogany's voice cracked, breaking the silence in the car. "I was just trying to break it up."

Mom's hands curled around the steering wheel. She turned to face Mahogany, and her stone expression cracked into a frown. "When did you get that fake hair weaved all into ya hair? And how did you pay for that?"

"Yesterday, after school," Mahogany whispered. "And I had been saving my allowance."

"You mean yesterday after school, when you were supposed to be studying for an exam at a friend's apartment?"

"Yes."

"So, you lied to me?"

"Yes." Mahogany's voice was barely audible. Mom tightened her grip on the steering wheel. "Since when did you start lying to me?" Mahogany slumped in her seat without answering. "I'll tell you when," Mom began, answering for her. "Ever since you started hanging out with that Karisma girl." Mahogany's eyes widened. Mom continued, "When Mr. Sullivan called me at work and told me you were fighting, I was in shock. I left immediately, and I was going to confront Mr. Sullivan when I arrived at school because I didn't believe him when he told me that my youngest daughter had been fighting. I just knew he was mistaken. Until I called Melani on my ride to the school. So, Melani tells me that for the past several weeks, you've been hanging out with that Karisma girl. And since you've been hanging out with her, you've been in two fights, you've lied to me, you skipped school at least one time, although Melani suspects it's more than that, and now you're suspended for five days." Mahogany's teeth gnawed into her bottom lip and her fingers curled into tight fists. She imagined those fists pounding on the sides of Melani's head for snitching. Mom continued, "So, after all of that, do you really expect me to believe you when you say you weren't fighting? That you were simply breaking up a fight?" Mom was squeezing the steering wheel so tight, Mahogany thought she might rip it off.

"But I wasn't—"

"Shut your mouth!" Mom bellowed in the car. Mahogany cringed. She never saw her mom so upset. "Don't say another word to me!" Mom demanded. "I need time to think of what I'm going to do to you." Mom started the ignition, and they pulled off in the direction of their building.

Chapter 11

You loved me before my name was hood famous, before the mix tape/
Before my crew of thugs, before I popped my first gun in the staircase/

A constant buzzing sound awakened Mahogany from her sleep. She rolled over and snatched her phone from the nightstand. *Why is Makai calling me at this time?* Mahogany thought, staring at her cell phone screen. "Hello," Mahogany croaked.

"Yo, Mahogany? Can you talk?" Makai asked, half out of breath.

"I'm not supposed to be," Mahogany said, now whispering. "Why are you calling me so late?"

"I just need a place to crash for the night. Can I come over?"

"Are you crazy!" Mahogany squealed in a loud whisper. "My mother won't even allow me to have boys over in the daylight. You think she's gonna let you come over here after midnight? And let you spend the night on top of that? You must be crazy."

"It's 12:15 right now. Ain't ya mom asleep?"

"I'm pretty sure she is."

"A'ight then. What she don't know won't hurt her."

"Are you tryna say you want me to sneak you in here?"

"Bingo!"

"Why do you need to come over right now? I thought we were supposed to meet up in the morning? After my mother and sister leave for work and school."

"Change of plans. I need to come over right now!"

"But why? I don't understand—"

"Mahogany! Listen! Tell me what you hear in the background?"

"Um…police sirens?" Mahogany answered, pressing the phone closer to her ear to get a better listen.

"Exactly. And they're looking for me. I need a place to hide, and your place is perfect because the police won't look for me there."

"Why are the cops looking for you?"

"I ain't got time to talk about that right now! I need a place to hide out! So can I come over or what?"

"I-I don't know."

"I thought you said you were down for me."

"I am down for you."

"A'ight then. So let me come over."

"But what if I get caught?"

"You won't. Trust me."

"Um—"

"Mahogany, do you hear how close them sirens are now? Do you want me to get arrested?"

"Of course not."

"Mahogany, I need you more than ever right now."

"Wait, hold on a minute," Mahogany said. After pressing the phone to her chest to smother the light, she slipped outside of her room and inched her mother's bedroom door open. Mahogany saw a huge lump under the sheets on the left side of her mom's bed. She studied the lump for a few seconds to see if it would move. It didn't. But it made strange chainsaw-like noises. Her mother had bad sinus problems and sounded like she was sawing logs when she slept. Mahogany knew right away that she was out like a broken streetlight. She reentered her bedroom and placed the phone back to her ear. "Okay," she gave in.

"A'ight, I'll be up there in two minutes."

Mahogany crept down the hall and pressed her ear to the apartment door. Her heart thumped when she heard the elevator door rumble open. Mahogany inhaled deeply through her nostrils and let the dead air escape, slowly, through her pursed lips before unlocking the door. She inched the door open just enough to poke out her head. Makai, who was wearing all black, moved from the elevator to Mahogany's door in a flash, cutting through the project hall like a shadow.

"My mother will kill me if she finds you in my room," Mahogany mentioned.

"She won't. Stop worrying." Mahogany stepped aside as Makai eased into the apartment. Quietly, she closed and locked the door. "Step where I step," Mahogany ordered. "The floor is really creaky." Mahogany crept along the wall on the balls of her toes, trying to take as much pressure off of the wooded tiles as she could. Makai followed closely behind. Just as she reached the doorway of her bedroom, the wood snapped beneath Makai's feet. They froze like burglars. Suddenly, light flooded into the hall from under her mother's door.

Quickly, Mahogany grabbed Makai by his arm and pushed open her bedroom door. Mom's bedroom door creaked open. Mahogany kicked off her slippers and slid under the sheets of her bed. Makai crawled to the other side of the bed and sank below. Mahogany's bedroom door crept open, and Mom stuck her head in.

"Mahogany, you up? I heard a noise."

"I didn't hear anything," Mahogany said while yawning.

"Must be the floor settling," Mom mentioned, her buggy eyes scanning the darkened room. She slowly backed out of the entrance and closed the door.

Mahogany waited about two minutes before rising up from the bed. "I think you should sleep in the closet," Mahogany whispered down to Makai.

"Sleep in the closet for what?" Makai asked in a voice that was louder than a whisper.

"Shhhh! My mother will hear you," Mahogany hissed.

"Why can't I just sleep right here?"

"What if my mother comes in here, in the morning, and sees you sleeping on the floor?"

The room was so obscure to Mahogany's eyes, it appeared as if Makai's shadow begrudgingly rose up from the floor and floated over to the closet. Carefully, Mahogany tiptoed to her closet and opened the door for Makai. "As soon as my mother and sister leave, I will let you right out, I promise." Makai stepped into the closet, and sat on the floor beside a pile of clothes. He hugged his knees to his chest since he couldn't stretch. Mahogany closed the closet door, sealing the darkness in with him.

Mahogany tossed and turned the rest of the night, looking for sleep. It was extremely hard to find a spot of comfort, especially knowing her mother could walk in at any moment.

Light slowly grew outside Mahogany's window while she eyed the door and listened for any noise coming from behind it. Every other minute, she turned toward her digital alarm clock, rooting for the red laser beams to form 7:30. By that time, her mother and sister would be out of the apartment, on their way to work and school. But every time she turned, it seemed as though 7:00 stared back at her.

Since the top two laser beams on her old digital clock were dull, the two zeros gave the appearance of the letter *u*. The more she stared at it though, the more it gave the appearance of two huge grins, taunting her.

The light in her room did more than just eat away at the darkness. It also seemed to devour the silence.

First, the sound of doors creaking open and closing. Running water, plates cracking against other plates in the dish rack, and popping hot grease were the next predictable sounds. Before long, the noise died down, but the aroma of bacon and eggs filled Mahogany's room.

The closet door inched open, slowly. Makai poked out his head. Mahogany waved to him to get back in but he ignored her gesture. Makai mouthed the words, "I'm hungry. I want some of that bacon."

Without warning, Mahogany's doorknob rattled and the door inched open. Mom stepped in. Makai ducked his head back. Mahogany's heart jumped. She stared at her mother, wide-eyed, hoping she didn't see him.

"Your teachers emailed me your school work for this week," Mom began. "I printed them out and its sitting on the love seat. Make sure you do some of your work today and clean up this room."

"Yes, Mom."

"And do the dishes as well."

"Yes, Mom."

"And I also left a Watchtower on top of your science text for you to read as well."

"Okay, Mom."

"Also, I received an email from your guidance counselor, Ms. Kanika Camara. She has invited you to attend the S.I.C.K program for five days when you get back. It's a new afterschool program at your school."

"Is it like a detention?"

"Not really. You *do* have to stay after school for an hour, but it's different from detention because the program offers remediation."

"You said they invited me. Does that mean I have a choice?"

"No, you do not have a choice," Mom demanded. "You are going! And—" Mom froze mid-sentence, her eyes fixed on something behind Mahogany. Mahogany's heart thumped in her chest. She said a quick prayer in her head, hoping she didn't spot Makai in the closet. Mahogany's eyes tried to follow the path of her mother's eyes. The path led her to the closet door, which was slightly open. Only darkness was peeking out. Mahogany sighed in relief until her mom said, "Give me your phone." Mahogany's cell phone was on her nightstand next to the bed, just in front of the closet. "I forgot to take that from you yesterday in the car." Mahogany handed Mom the phone and watched her walk out of the room.

After a few more minutes, the running water and smell of bacon were replaced by the click-clacking of stiletto pumps and the scent of perfume. Soon after, Mahogany heard the front door of the apartment open and slam shut. Mahogany jumped out of the bed, removed the condom from her nightstand drawer, and scurried into the bathroom. Behind the locked bathroom door, Mahogany held the silver plastic wrap of the condom before her eyes. A sense of guilt overwhelmed her. It fell from her fingers and onto the sink as if it were on fire in her hand.

Mahogany shook the thoughts of the condom from her mind like cobwebs before getting into her routine. She discarded her scarf, combed her new Brazilian, washed her face, and then twisted open the top of the brand new jar of skin-bleaching cream she bought the day before. After rubbing the cream onto her face, she stared at the mirror as if she were trying to watch her skin lighten before her eyes. She darted back into her bedroom and locked the door behind her. "You can come out now. We're finally alone." Makai limped out of the closet and collapsed on the bed, massaging his legs.

"Now hook me up with some of that bacon," Makai demanded.

"You didn't say anything about my hair," Mahogany mentioned, smiling and posing. "Do you like it?"

"It's dope," Makai said, rubbing his belly. "It looks good on you. Now where's the bacon? I'm starvin'." Mahogany didn't bother to hide her disappointment while stepping into her slippers and out of her room. When she entered the kitchen, she was startled to find Melani standing in front of the stove with a piece of tissue stuffed in her right nostril and a blue mug in her hand. Melani's petite frame was shivering under a purple blanket.

"What you still doing here?" Mahogany asked. Melani turned and exploded into a frenzy of coughing and gagging. "I'm not feeling well," Melani complained. Mahogany was steaming more than the pot of water Melani was pouring into her mug.

"So, I guess that means you're not going to school today?" Melani shook her head and dunked a teabag into the mug. Mahogany cursed under her breath. She tuned and marched down the hall and back into the room. Makai sat up, staring into Mahogany's empty hands.

"Where's the bacon?"

"Shhh! Lower your voice. My sister's home." Mahogany grabbed her remote and turned on the television, hoping to drown out their conversation.

"What she gotta do with the bacon?"

"We got bigger problems."

"Problems like what? She ate all of the bacon?"

"No. The problem is, she's sick, so she's staying home from school today. If she hears you or sees you, that's my butt, because she will definitely tell my mother."

"You mean to tell me your own sister will snitch on you?"

"In a heartbeat. So you gotta be super quiet and you gotta hide."

"I ain't gettin' back in that closet," Makai said, massaging his legs again.

"You don't have to. Just get down on the side of the bed, just in case she tries to come in here."

"A'ight. Just go get my bacon," Makai demanded, settling on the floor beside the bed.

Seconds after Makai chewed up the dried bacon and scraps of scrambled eggs Mom left behind for breakfast, he was licking ketchup off his fingers and asking for more.

"I can't go back out there and get more food."

"Why?"

"Cause, I don't eat like that, and if my sister sees me getting more food, she might get suspicious."

"Hide it or something. I'm still hungry."

Melani was curled up on the couch watching television, so Mahogany knew she would be alone in the kitchen. Mahogany didn't bother to check the cabinet because she knew there wasn't any more bread. She opened the fridge and removed four slices of honey turkey meat from a ziplock bag. Mahogany spread mayonnaise on top of the turkey meat, folded it, and stuffed it in her pajama pocket.

"Here," Mahogany said, handing Makai the turkey meat.

"What am I'm supposed to do with this?"

"Eat it."

"Where's the bread? Where's the mayo?"

"We ain't got no more bread and the mayo is in the middle."

"This is so ghetto," Makai remarked before shoving the honey turkey roll into his mouth.

"I want to show you something," Mahogany said, reaching for her drawing pad on her nightstand. She flipped through a few pages and placed the opened drawing pad in Makai's hands. Makai's eyes traced the sketch of a boy whose eyes were peeking through the bars of his window.

"Wow, this is a really good drawing. You did this?"

"Yeah. I drew it about a year ago."

"You got a lot of talent."

"Thank you."

"Wait a minute," Makai said, scanning the picture again. "Is this supposed to be me?"

"Yeah," Mahogany replied.

"It kinda looks like I'm in prison."

"So you *get it.* That was my vision. When I used to see you looking out of your window, it looked as if you were trapped behind the window bars, and your sad eyes were hoping that someone would release you so you could join the boys on the corner."

"Well, as you can see, I no longer watch the boys on the block from my window anymore. Now, I am one of the boys on the block."

"How did that happen?"

"Whatchu mean?"

"How did you go from the window to the block?"

"I kinda didn't have a choice." Makai paused, cleared his throat, and continued. "About a month ago, I was on my way home from the corner store when I ran into Sleep and Angel hanging out in my building lobby. We didn't know each other yet, so they cornered me by the mailboxes and was about to rob me. They thought I lived on the Northside. When I told them I lived in that building, they said either I roll with them or get rolled on. That's when I saw Sleep tuck his hand in his jacket like he was going for a gun or something, and I didn't want to get *rolled on,* so—"

"So they forced you to be down with them?"

"Not really."

"But they threatened you!"

"True. But I used to daydream about being down with them when I used to watch them from my window."

"You remind me of someone I know."

"Who?"

"A friend from my past," Mahogany said, then changed the subject. "But help me understand. Why did they need you to be down with them?"

"Because they got beef with the Northside, and Sleep said the Southside need more soldiers."

"Soldiers for what?"

"For war. Against the Northside."

"Why is the Southside beefin' with the Northside?" Before Makai could respond, the sound of a siren rang out just on the other side of Mahogany's bedroom window. Makai jumped up and peered out the window until the sound of the sirens became a mere echo. He slumped down into a seat just below the window with his back against the cold radiator. His shoulders and head slumped down as well.

"So, are you ready to tell me what happened last night?" Mahogany asked softly, taking a seat on the edge of the bed. Makai squirmed in his seat as if he were struggling to get the words out.

"Remember Donovan? The big dude I introduced you to at the hooky party?" Makai asked, voice barely above a whisper.

"Yeah, I remember him," Mahogany responded, turning down the volume on the television with the remote so she could hear Makai.

"Well, last night, he knocked on my door and asked me to go with him to handle something right quick. I knew something was wrong because he had this crazy, deranged look on his face. Normally, when Donovan says 'handle something,' he's talking about beatin' someone up or robbin' them. I never 'handled' anything with Donovan before, so I thought it was strange that he was asking me to go with him. So, I asked him why me and why not one of the Yardie boys. And—"

"Yardie boys?"

"The Yardie boys is a crew of Jamaican dudes that Donovan is down with. Dready, who is the leader, his brother Zion, Donovan, and Bigga. Anyway, as I was saying, when I asked him why didn't he ask one of his Yardie boys crew, he said I was the only one that answered the door. So, I followed him over to the Northside, and as we were walking, I saw a gun handle poking out of the top of his pants. The sight of the gun scared me, and I was like, 'Yo, whatchu about to do with that gun?' And he said, 'About to get my revenge on Tafari.'"

"Tafari!" Mahogany gasped.

"Yeah, you know him?" Makai asked, studying Mahogany's face. "You said his name like you know him."

"Umm…yeah…kind of," Mahogany stammered. "We went to church together. So, did Donovan…umm…did he…"

"No, he didn't shoot Tafari."

"Thank God!" Mahogany sighed.

"He shot someone else," Makai murmured, eyeing the floor.

"Who?"

"Let me finish tellin' the story. So, we stopped at the corner, directly across the street from the deli on the Northside. We saw two guys chillin' right in front of the entrance. At that point, I told Donovan that I ain't down with shootin' nobody. I was about to turn around and leave, but then Donovan flashed the gun in my face and said, 'You ain't goin' nowhere!' I ain't even gon' front, I was scared to death. I ain't never had a gun in my face before. I froze right on the spot. Then, he turned and looked at the two dudes across the street and said, 'Yo, I think that's him right there!' I said, 'Yo, that ain't Tafari!' He said, 'Yes it is. This is where he hangs out!' And I said, 'Trust me, that ain't him. I know who that is.' Either Donovan didn't hear me or he just ignored me. Next thing I know, what sounded like three thunderclaps roared from Donovan's gun. Bah! Bah! Bah! Yo, them gunshots scared the life outta me. The one who Donovan thought was Tafari dropped like a sandbag, and the other dude took off running down the block. Donovan yelled, 'I got 'em, let's go!' and we took off running. We ran all the way over here to the Southside until we reached Donovan's building. We hid in the staircase for a while until Donovan said we need to split up. He told me not to go home because if the cops came looking for us, that's the first place they would look. He shoved the gun in my hand and told me to hide it. Then, he took off running down the stairs, and that's the last time I saw him. Right after he left, I called you."

"You still didn't tell me who Donovan shot?"

Makai hesitated. "It was...Timothy."

"Timothy Morgan?" Mahogany wondered.

"Yeah, you know him too?"

"He used to go to the same church that I used to go to. How do you know him?"

"I don't, or I didn't. I mean, we were in the same geography class, and we may have said 'what's up' to each other a couple of times, but I didn't know him personally. But either way, Timothy didn't deserve to go out like that. He was...he was just standing there."

"Is he...is he dead?"

"I'm not sure, but I would be surprised if he survived." Makai hung his head and used his fingertips to dry the corners of his eyes again.

"What about the dude that was with Timothy? Did you see who it was?"

"I'm not one hundred percent, but it looked like Amir."

"Amir?!"

"Why you say his name like that? Don't tell me you know *him* too?"

"No, no, it's just that, um—"

"Just that what?"

"I saw him on Instagram recently, that's all."

"Between me and you, I'm scared, Mahogany," Makai revealed. "I don't know what I'm gonna do."

Makai was still sitting by the window, but through his eyes, Mahogany could see that his mind was somewhere else. Probably back at the crime scene. Mahogany's mind was at the crime scene too. Tafari was there. Feelings she had for Tafari that she thought were buried deep within began to resurface. The thought of him being killed had her stomach doing somersaults. An overflow of memories that she shared with Tafari flooded her mind.

A thick cloud of depression descended onto Mahogany's bedroom. The mood in the room made it obvious to Mahogany that what was supposed to go down in the bedroom *was not going to go down*. The point of Mahogany and Makai linking up again was to give Mahogany a chance to do over what she couldn't do with Makai at the hooky party. The way things were looking, they were not going to do the *do-over.* And Mahogany wasn't unhappy about that. Actually, she was relieved.

Chapter 12

Beat down wit' fists and words and/ sometimes it feels like livin' is worthless/
When ya losing ya identity and forgettin' ya purpose/

B*ang! Bang! Bang!* "Who are you talking to in there?!" Melani yelled out while banging on the door. "It sounds like you're talking to someone!"

"I ain't talking to anyone," Mahogany yelled back. "You're hearing the television." Mahogany and Makai sat in silence, listening to Melani's footsteps as she crept away from the bedroom door.

All of a sudden, a song with banging 808s and stuttering hi-hats rang out from Makai's cell phone. "Cut that off, quick, before my sister hears it!" Mahogany demanded. Quickly, Makai pulled the phone from his pocket and silenced it. Over the next ten minutes, the cell phone vibrated in Makai's hand, and he ignored every call. "Who keeps calling you?" Mahogany asked.

"It's Donovan."

"Why don't you answer it?"

"I…I can't talk to him right now," Makai stammered. "I need to clear my head."

"Maybe he just wants to see how you doin'."

"You wanna know how I'm doin'? I'm going crazy. I need to get outta here!"

"Shhhhh!" Mahogany hushed, finger over her lips.

"I gotta go." Makai stood up and reached for the small black bag he brought with him.

"You can't right now. I told you my sister is out there. If she sees you, she's gonna tell my mother."

"So what am I supposed to do?"

"We gonna have to wait until tonight when everyone is asleep." And that's exactly what they did. Waited. Her mom arrived home a little after seven. Makai hid in the closet until close to midnight when Mahogany allowed him to crawl out. "My mom and sister are finally asleep," Mahogany whispered.

"About time. It felt like I was in there forever," Makai complained in a loud whisper, kicking the kinks out of his legs.

"Okay, let's go," Mahogany urged.

"Wait. I need you to do two things for me."

"Two things like what?"

"First, I need you to hide something for me."

"What do you want me to hide?" Makai handed Mahogany the small black bag he had brought with him the night before. "What's in here?" Mahogany asked.

"It's a gun."

"What?!" Now it was Makai's turn to shush Mahogany.

"It's Donovan's gun. Just hide it for me."

"I can't. Take this thing with you," Mahogany pleaded.

"What if *them boys* are right outside?"

"*Them boys?*"

"The cops. What if they snatch me up as soon as I step foot outside this building? If they catch me with that gun, it's over for me."

"I don't know about this."

"You want me to get arrested and locked in jail forever?" Mahogany shook her head.

"A'ight then. Just hide it for me, and I promise I will come back for it real soon." Mahogany took the bag from Makai. The room was so dark that her hands had to do the seeing for her. Mahogany clutched the bag with her left hand, stuck her right hand out, and felt for the closet doorknob. After opening the closet door, Mahogany kneeled down and placed the bag with the gun under a pile of dirty clothes.

"A'ight, I need you to do one last thing for me," Makai said, still whispering.

"Oh God," Mahogany whispered, bracing herself for Makai's next request.

"I'm not going home tonight. I'm going to lay low at my aunt's house for a couple of days, so I need a ride over to Co-op City."

"And what do you want me to do?"

"Let me borrow ya mom's car."

"You must be crazy."

"I know how to drive. Plus, Co-op City is only like ten minutes away. It's late and there ain't gonna be many cars on the road. It'll be an easy drive."

"Why can't you just call a cab?"

"I ain't got cab money. You got cab money?"

"No."

"A'ight then. That's why I need ya mom's car."

"Even if I did let you borrow my mom's car, how would we get the car back in time for my mom to drive to work in the morning?"

"I'll drop myself off and you can drive it back."

"I don't know how to drive."

"Ya friend Ya Ya can drive. I saw her driving Karisma to the mall one day after school. I'll text her."

"Wait a minute," Mahogany said. Before Mahogany could get in another word, Makai looked up from his phone.

"She said she'll do it."

"Do what?"

"Drive with us over to Co-op and then drive you back home."

"But—"

"She just said Karisma is down to come too. They'll be downstairs in ten minutes. Let's go." By the time Mahogany could fully process what was going on, she was sitting in the passenger seat of her mom's car as Makai started the ignition and Ya Ya and Karisma settled in the back.

Co-op City was just that. A small city unto itself. An endless cluster of towering beige buildings piercing the night's midnight-blue sky. The car slowed almost to a halt as it rolled over the unusually massive speed bump, which looked more like a concrete hill that sat in the middle of the street.

"I appreciate you holdin' me down these last two nights, Mahogany," Makai said as the car pulled up to the curb in front of building fourteen. "I know it wasn't easy for you. You showed and proved that you are really down for me. I won't forget that. I luh you." Warm chills waterfalled down the back of Mahogany's neck and spine when Makai leaned over and slowly kissed her on the lips. Her body remained slightly tilted, lips still poked out, frozen in a kissing pose even seconds after Makai exited the car and headed toward the building.

Ya Ya circled around to the front of the car and settled into the driver's seat. "Did y'all hear that? Makai said he loves me!" Mahogany beamed.

"Forget that," Karisma squealed from the back seat. "Girl! Makai just spent a night in your room! Tell us all the juicy details!"

"There ain't no juicy details."

"Whatchu mean?"

"There's nothing to tell you because nothing happened."

"Don't tell me you fronted on him and chickened out again?"

"No. It wasn't me this time."

"What?! So, you're saying he didn't want to *do it*?"

"He had a lot on his mind."

"What could have possibly been on his mind other than getting in a girl's pants? Because that's all guys think about," Ya Ya chimed in.

"Well, I imagine being on the run from the cops and worrying about being arrested might make it hard to think about anything else."

"Why is he on the run from the cops?" Karisma asked.

"Because Donovan shot someone the other night."

"Oh my God! Who did Donovan shoot?" Ya Ya gasped.

"A boy named Timothy Morgan."

"What does that have to do with Makai?" Karisma asked.

"Makai was with Donovan when he shot him."

"Why did Donovan shoot him?" Ya Ya asked.

"Remember when we were all at Makai's apartment and they were clowning Donovan about not doing anything when Tafari took his girl's chain?"

"Yeah."

"Well, Donovan finally decided to do something about it. He went looking for Tafari, but he shot the wrong person. Makai called me later on that night and begged me to let him stay the night with me because he was afraid the cops were looking for him and Donovan. He hid in my room for two nights, and now, he's going to hide out at his aunt's apartment."

"Did the boy he shot die?"

"I don't know," Mahogany said in a low voice.

"Dag, it's gonna be crazy around the way now," Karisma admitted. "Cops are gonna be all over the block and all up in the schools looking for suspects. Rio and them ain't gonna be makin' no money for a while."

"It's funny you say that because at the hooky party, I heard Angel say that him and Rio were missing out on money by not being in school. So how do they make their money?"

"Is she serious?" Karisma joked with Ya Ya.

"What's so funny?" Mahogany asked.

"How do you think they make their money?"

"I don't know, that's why I asked." Mahogany shrugged.

"Come on. Do you notice how fly Rio and Angel dress? Where do you think they get their money from?"

"Drugs? Is it from drugs?"

"Ding! Ding! Ding! Ding! Ding!"

"I had no idea that people were dealing drugs in school," Mahogany revealed. "I thought Bronx High was one of the better schools in the area."

"It seems like there's a lot of things you don't have any idea about." Ya Ya laughed.

"What is that supposed to mean?"

"You're naïve, boo-boo."

"Take that back!" Mahogany snapped.

"Why?"

"Because I'm not stupid."

"That's not what I meant when I called you naïve," Ya Ya responded, accent dripping with Spanish flavor. "I just mean that you're innocent. Like, you don't have much experience with the real world outside of your room and the Kingdom Hall."

"You sound like my ex. He used to say that I don't know what's real in the streets."

"Forget the streets; you don't even know what's *real* in our school." Karisma laughed. "Why do you think people call our school Hard Knocks High?"

"I didn't know people called our school Hard Knocks High," Mahogany disclosed. Karisma and Ya Ya laughed again. "What's so funny?"

"Like I said, you're naïve...um...I mean innocent."

"Well, I don't want to be innocent anymore. So tell me why they call our school Hard Knocks High?"

"Like I said, people selling, buying, and using drugs in the school—"

"Gangs, fights, and crazy teachers," Karisma added.

"Does Makai sell drugs too?"

"Nah. And he won't be anytime soon. He better hope the cops don't find him over here."

"Look, can we talk and drive at the same time?" Mahogany urged. "We need to hurry up and get my mother's car back."

"I still can't believe Donovan shot someone," Ya Ya said as she put the car in drive and smashed on the gas, half paying attention to the road. "I could tell that Donovan was upset when we were in Makai's apartment, but I never thought—"

"Ya Ya, slow down! Watch out for that big speed bump!" Mahogany yelled. The front wheels of the car plowed into the enormous speed bump and vaulted into the air, slamming violently back onto the street. The car jerked to the right, jumped the curb, and rammed into the metal light pole on the corner. Mahogany opened her eyes and wondered why her cheeks were burning, until she saw a deployed airbag deflated in front of her. She turned to her left and noticed a deflated air bag dangling out of the steering wheel in front of Ya Ya as well. Ya Ya didn't seem to notice. Something on the other side of the windshield seemed to have Ya Ya spooked, the way her eyes were bugging from their sockets. Mahogany followed Ya Ya's line of vision and was alarmed to see steam spraying out from under either side of the half-opened hood.

"I smell gas!" Ya Ya shrieked. She panicked, popped the door open, and took off running down the block.

"Let's get outta here!" Karisma yelled and took off running behind Ya Ya. Mahogany snatched the keys from the ignition and ran after Karisma and Ya Ya.

The girls ran, jogged, and fast-walked all the way back to the projects in half an hour. Mahogany made it into her bedroom unnoticed. She crawled into her bed and searched for sleep but never found it. Each time she sealed her eyelids shut, the car crash replayed itself over and over in her mind's eye.

It was almost 7:30 in the morning when Mahogany heard Mom yelling in the kitchen. Usually, Mom would leave a little after seven, and Mahogany and Melani would have the apartment to themselves for at least a half hour before they left for school. But Mom was still there. And she was upset.

Slowly, Mahogany crept into the kitchen and saw Mom sitting at the head of the kitchen table. She was dressed for work: navy blue business suit and black high heels. Her car keys were in her right hand and her cell phone was in her left, pressed to her ear. "Yes, this is the number I was told to call to report a stolen car!" Melani, who was wrapped in the same purple blanket from the morning before, sat opposite Mom at the kitchen table. She glared at Mahogany when she entered the kitchen. Mahogany rolled her eyes at Melani and focused back on Mom. "So, I parked my car last night at 7:30, just across the street from my building. Ten minutes ago, I walked out to my car so I can go to work, and it was gone." Mom listened for a few seconds and detonated. "I'm not crazy! I know exactly where I parked my car! It's not there anymore!" Mom listened again and detonated again. "Yes, I have kids, but my girls are good girls, and they would never take my car without permission. Besides, I have the car keys in my hand. So, are you gonna send a cop out here so I can file a report or what?" Mahogany's stomach sank as she listened to Mom yell into the phone. She had never seen her mom so angry, and it was all because of something she did.

Melani glared at Mahogany like she knew something. Like she knew what Mahogany did. Or maybe Mahogany's mind was playing tricks on her. Mahogany dragged herself back to bed and wept until she found the sleep she was looking for.

Chapter 13

Blacks come in different flavas/ we're the Baskin Robbins of races/ Caramel swirl, butter pecan and chocolate faces/

The bell blared through the halls and classrooms of Bronx High, indicating the end of the school day. While students were hurrying through the exits, Mahogany met up with Karisma by the gym. "Oh my God! Karisma, your hair! You look so good!" Mahogany chanted, a mix of shock, surprise, and satisfaction in her voice.

"You like it?" Karisma asked, twisting her neck from side to side so Mahogany could see the back.

"Yeeeees! It looks so nice! When did you get it done?"

"Yesterday. When I saw how beautiful you looked and all the attention you were getting, I decided to get my hair done just like yours."

"You know, I'm mad atchu, Karisma!"

"Why are you mad at me?"

"As good as you look right now witcha hair done, you coulda been took off that scarf."

"I thought about doing this a while ago, but it wasn't until I saw how good you looked when you got your hair done that I got the confidence to do it too."

Mahogany continued to compliment Karisma as they walked against the crowd of exiting students, following signs for the S.I.C.K. meeting. "There it is, right there," Karisma said, pointing down the hall. "The meeting is in the band room."

"Who is that standing in the doorway?" Mahogany asked.

"That's Mr. Sekou," Karisma answered. "He's one of the tenth-grade English teachers. He is sooo fine. I wish I was in his class." As the girls approached the band room, they were greeted by Mr. Sekou.

"Welcome, ladies. I'm Mr. Sharif Sekou." Mr. Sekou smiled, extending his hand to shake theirs. "And your names are?"

"My name is Karisma James, and this is Mahogany Brown."

"Okay," Mr. Sekou responded, checking their names off on the list he held on a clipboard. "You ladies can have a seat. We will get started in a few minutes." Mr. Sekou stepped aside, allowing the girls to enter. Mahogany noticed three boys already sitting in seats one by the window on the far right, one close to the door in the front reading a book, and the other sitting in the middle.

"Hey Karisma," the boy by the window called out.

"Whassup, Myles?" Karisma called back, walking toward the back of the band room with Mahogany following closely behind.

"Oh snap! Karisma took her scarf off!" said the boy in the middle row.

"And! You gotta problem with that, Big Snacks?" Karisma paused and bucked at the boy with her hands balled into tight fists.

"Nah, just that, you look good!"

"That's what I thought." Karisma and Mahogany continued to the back and took a seat.

"So, whatchu in here for?" Big Snacks asked, turning around in his seat.

"I had a fight."

"Dang, girl. You stay fightin'."

"And I stay winnin' too. These chicks gon' learn to stop messin' wit me."

"I here you, champ." At that point, everyone's eyes averted to the door as a boy strolled through the entrance.

"Oh my God! He looks sooo good," Karisma whispered, eyes wide with desire.

"You ain't lyin', girl," Mahogany agreed.

"I would love to run my fingers through his soft curly hair while staring into his hypnotizing hazel eyes."

"What did you say?" Mahogany giggled.

"That boy got me spittin' poetry over here." Karisma laughed, fanning herself.

Myles and Big Snacks were staring in awe at the boy, as if a celebrity had just entered the band room.

"Peace, Milk," said the boy who was reading the book.

"What up, Sha'King?"

"What's good, Milk?" Big Snacks cheered.

"I'm Gucci," Milk responded.

"Speaking of Gucci, I'm feelin' that Gucci belt."

"Appreciate it, my guy." Milk and Big Snacks bumped fists before Milk took a seat right beside Myles.

"Yo, Milk, where you get them Jays from? I never seen them sneakers in that color before," Myles asked.

"Chill, Myles. You know I can't tell you the spot I be coppin' my sneakers at. If I tell you, then you gonna tell somebody else. Next thing you know, the whole school is gonna be bitin' my style."

"Yo, I promise I won't tell nobody else."

"I'll think about it."

"A'ight. Oh, yeah, I just got a job at the barbershop. So, if you need a cut, come through and I'll hook you up."

"Good lookin' out, my G." At that point, Mr. Sekou entered the band room with Zuri and Imani walking cautiously alongside him. They spotted the girls in the back and decided to take a seat up front, close to Mr. Sekou, where it was safe. Karisma sneered at their presence. Another girl, wearing a black hoodie, walked in and slid into a seat right in front of Big Snacks.

"Is that Noni?" Karisma asked Mahogany, a hint of shock in her voice. "What in the world could she have done to end up here?"

"I can't imagine her fighting or even getting in trouble because she's so quiet."

"Like they say, it's the quiet ones you have to look out for."

"Good afternoon, students," Mr. Sekou said, interrupting the quiet conversations in the room.

"Good afternoon," several students murmured.

"First off, I want to say welcome to our returning students. As for our new students, I want to say welcome. I'm Mr. Sekou, one of the tenth-grade English teachers here at Bronx High, and I am also the founder of the S.I.C.K program. In case any of our new students in here are wondering, this program is designed for at-risk teens in this school who may have gotten into trouble. This program allows you guys an opportunity to discuss your problems with someone who can not only understand you, but will remediate and come up with solutions to help prevent you guys from getting into trouble again—" Mr. Sekou paused as Ms. Camara opened the door and entered the band room.

"Hey guys, sorry I'm late," Ms. Camara apologized, walking across the room and placing her bag on the teacher's desk.

"Perfect timing," Mr. Sekou said to Ms. Camara before turning his attention back to the students. "As of today, Ms. Camara has been added as a mentor in the S.I.C.K. program. Actually, she will facilitate this afternoon's session because I have to leave in a few minutes. As all of us are aware, we recently lost a Bronx High student, Timothy Morgan, to gun violence. Timothy was one of my students, and his parents are having a vigil at his apartment this afternoon. I was asked to attend. Right after the vigil, I will go directly to the hospital to visit another one of my students, Tafari King, who was shot last night."

"Did you say Tafari King?" Mahogany gasped.

"Yes. He was shot last night. Fortunately, his injuries aren't life threatening. I, along with Big Snacks, Myles, and Sha'King, visited him last night. He seems to be doing okay. Now, with that said, I will turn the floor over to Ms. Camara." Before Ms. Camara spoke to the class, she and Mr. Sekou stepped out into the hallway and had a brief discussion before Mr. Sekou left for the rest of the afternoon.

Mahogany pulled out her phone and texted Tafari, asking if he was okay. She also sent a text to her mom, asking her if she had heard about Tafari being shot.

"I can't believe Tafari got shot," Mahogany whispered to Karisma. Karisma didn't respond because she was staring and seething at Zuri and Imani.

"Karisma?" Mahogany whispered again, nudging Karisma with her elbow.

"Huh? Whatchu say?"

"I said, I can't believe Tafari got shot."

"Who's Tafari?" Karisma asked. "I don't know him."

"He's the one that Donovan was trying to shoot, but he mistakenly shot Timothy instead, 'member?"

Still ignoring Mahogany, Karisma popped out of her seat and barked at the girls in the front of the class. "Ayo, I know y'all ain't up there talkin' 'bout me!"

"Ain't nobody talking about you," Imani snapped. "You always ear-hustling. Matter of fact, ain't nobody even thinking about you. Girl, bye!"

"Don't be girl-byeing me! I'll come up there and slap you right in ya Lite-Brite-face!"

"And I'll slap you right across ya black face!"

"Ladies! Ladies! Calm down!" Ms. Camara yelled as she stormed back into the band room. "Karisma! Sit down!"

"This ain't over!" Karisma shouted before begrudgingly easing back into her seat.

"No, it is over, Karisma!"

"Did you hear what she said to me?" Karisma asked. "She called me black."

"Only after you called me Lite-Brite," Imani retorted.

"Ladies, we all come in different shades and colors. That's what makes our race so beautiful," Ms. Camara reasoned.

"The fact that we come in different shades of brown is one of the biggest problems that we face," Sha'King said, lowering the book he was reading.

"What is your name, young man?"

"Sha'King Mosely, ma'am."

"So, what do you mean by that statement, Sha'King?"

"We as black people were tricked to believe that light is right and black is ugly. We were taught to hate our natural skin color, our heritage, and ourselves. That's why dark-skinned blacks hate on light-skinned blacks and vice versa. It's a divide and conquer tactic that started during slavery—"

"Don't tell me you blaming all of our problems on slavery?" Big Snacks shouted, hands in the air. "Why we always gotta go back there?"

"Because it's true, my brother," Sha'King began. "We were pitted against each other from the start. House slaves vs. field slaves; light-skinned vs. dark-skinned; short hair vs. long hair. Instead of embracing the differences that make our race so unique and beautiful, we hate on each other and remain divided because we don't know the truth about who we really are and where we really come from."

"We come from slavery. Everybody knows that," Myles shrugged.

"That's not true," Sha'King corrected. "Before we were forced to come over here as slaves, a lot of us lived lavishly in Africa as queens and kings. King Hannibal, King Mansa Musa, Queen Nefertiti, Empress Candace, and a bunch more. We were also scholars too, in a land called Timbuktu in Africa, which had the first libraries and universities. Greeks and people from all over the world would travel to Timbuktu to study and learn. That is a part of our history way before slavery. The more we know about ourselves, the more we will love ourselves and not hate on each other."

"This here is a sermon of truth!" Zuri shouted from the front of the class. "You better preach, my brother!"

"How you know all this stuff?" Big Snacks asked, staring at Sha'King as if he were a young prodigy.

"By reading," Sha'King announced, holding up the paperback book he was reading. "I also learned a lot from my older brother, Young Marcus, and this wise brother from around the way that we call Knowledge."

"Knowledge!" Myles called out. "You talkin' 'bout that crazy old-head that be walking around the projects, preaching on the corners and in the barbershop?"

"He ain't crazy!" Sha'King protested. "There's a fine line between crazy and genius, and he's a genius in my eyes. If you took the time to listen to him speak, you would find out that he speaks the truth and be droppin' jewelz."

"He'll steal ya jewels too if you don't keep your eyes on him." Big Snacks laughed. "He always be asking somebody for a dollar."

"Well, I have to admit, as a dark-brown-skinned woman, I have dealt with bouts of self-hate and not wanting to be dark when I was younger," Ms. Camara admitted, interrupting the boys' chatter. "But it wasn't until I learned to ignore what the ignorant world around me had to say that I learned how to truly love myself and embrace my heritage. But with that said, when you are dark-skinned, it's not easy growing up in a world where color matters, as Sha'King mentioned."

"It ain't easy growing up light-skinned either," Milk revealed.

"Mr. Deionte Parker," Ms. Camara announced, addressing Milk by his government name. "Would you mind elaborating on what you mean by that statement?"

"People think just because I'm light-skinned that I'm soft or I'm weak. When I was younger, some of my so-called friends who were darker than me used to tease me and say that I was as light as milk. I laughed with them while they were cracking jokes on me, but when I got home, I was really hurt by it. They had me not wanting to be light-skinned—"

"To be honest, bruh," Big Snacks interrupted. "You look more like eggnog. Yeah, we should call you eggnog." Big Snacks and Myles laughed.

"This is not the time for jokes, Trevor!" Ms. Camara denounced.

"Big Snacks, Ms. Camara. Call me Big Snacks," He insisted, while stuffing his mouth with a handful of mini chocolate chip cookies. "Mr. Sekou said its okay if we use our nicknames in here. He said it will make us feel more comfortable."

"Okay," Ms. Camara nodded. "Continue, Deionte."

"As I was sayin', when I got older, I decided to stop feeling sorry for myself. I decided to stand up for myself. And that's how I ended up here."

"Share with the class how you got into trouble, Deionte."

"You can call me Milk. I've embraced the name now, so I'm cool wit' it."

"Okay, Milk, share with the class why you were assigned to this program."

"So, it started when this girl started following me on Instagram. She was likin' all my pics and making comments that I was cute. Then she started sliding into my DMs and—"

"What does DM mean?" Ms. Camara asked.

"Direct message," Milk answered.

"It goes down in the DM," Big Snacks sang. Everyone erupted with laughter.

"Okay, okay, calm down, everyone." Ms. Camara chuckled. "Milk, continue."

"Okay, so, yeah, as I was sayin', the girl's boyfriend found out that his girl was sliding into my DMs, asking me for my number, and he ain't like it. So, last week, he followed me into Mr. Abraham's class and said I better leave his girl alone. I said, 'She's the one stalkin' me, so you need to check ya girl.' Then he started calling me soft and said ain't no way a light-skinned pretty boy could beat him up. The dude was clownin' me in front of my friends. So, I showed him that this light-skinned kid ain't soft. I stepped to him, two-pieced him in the face, then scooped him up and slammed him on top of the desk. After that, a couple of teachers from across the hall rushed into the room and broke it up."

"Mr. Abraham didn't break it up?" Myles wondered.

"Nah, he just sat there."

"Mr. Abraham don't do jack. He barely gives any work, he doesn't discipline anybody, he doesn't break up fights—you gotta love Mr. Abraham's class," Big Snacks chuckled.

"Earlier, you said that you didn't want to be light-skinned anymore. Is that true, Milk?" Sha'King asked with disbelief in his voice.

"Yeah, at one point I didn't. But when I got a little older, the girls started noticing me. They love my light skin and my curly Temp fade. So now, when it comes to being light-skinned, I'm like McDonalds."

"How are you like McDonalds, Milk?" Ms. Camara asked.

"I'm lovin' it!" The class erupted with laughter again.

"There are times when I hate being light-skinned too," Imani mentioned. "Especially when boys be like, 'Yo, yo redbone, comere!' I ain't no redbone!"

"We call all light-skinned chicks redbone," Myles acknowledged.

"Well, I don't like it."

"I wish dudes would say 'Yo, yo, redbone, comere' to me," Mahogany admitted. "Matter of fact, I wish they would just say 'comere.'"

"Well, it's annoying when them low-life boys on the corner be harassing girls all day," Imani responded, looking at Mahogany.

"I can't relate."

"You can't relate?" Big Snacks questioned. "But you're pretty—"

"Go 'head and say it!" Karisma interrupted.

"Say what!"

"That she's pretty for a dark-skinned girl!"

"I wasn't gonna say—"

"It's what everyone says," Karisma said, cutting him off again. "Why can't we be pretty, period!"

"But you are pretty," Ms. Camara assured. "As we all are. Light-skinned, dark—"

"Why you gotta say we all are?" Karisma huffed. "Why you gotta include light-skinned people? Everybody knows that light-skinned people are pretty—"

"Not all of 'em. I've seen some butt-ugly light-skinned girls before," Big Snacks joked.

"Watch ya mouth in here, boy!" Ms. Camara snapped.

"As I was saying," Karisma continued. "Why couldn't you just let what I said about dark-skinned people breathe on its own."

"But we are all pretty, regardless of color," Zuri added.

"You're not wrong, Zuri. But I do get where Karisma is coming from," Ms. Camara answered.

"The problem with most of us, especially those of us who are dark-skinned, is that we don't have any self-confidence," Sha'King added. "When I was younger and before I got knowledge of self, I would have given anything to be light-skinned. My older brother, Young Marcus, is light-brown-skinned, and so is my younger brother, Jahlil. Sometimes when my family was talking about me and my brothers, they would call me the black one. I started hating the way I looked until one day my granddad pulled me aside and showed me some pictures of himself when he was in his early twenties. He was actually a little darker than me. In every single picture, he had a different woman on his arms. My granddad said that it's all about having confidence in yourself because women love a confident man. So that's what I did. I stopped feeling sorry for myself because I wasn't light-skinned and embraced me for who I was. That was also the time when I started learning about the real history of black people and who we really are and where we really come from. The more I learned, the more I loved myself, and I try to encourage anyone that is dark-brown-skinned to embrace their skin color because like my granddad told me, 'black is beautiful.'"

"Amen, brother!" Ms. Camara praised.

"Actually, I can relate to what Milk said about not wanting to be light-skinned at one point," Zuri said, joining the conversation. "The same dark-skinned people that are embracing their skin color are the same ones…well, not all of them, but a lot of them hate on me for being light-skinned. It's like they are being racist toward me."

"How can a black person be prejudiced against another black person?" Myles wondered. "That don't make no sense."

"It makes a lot of sense, my brother," Zuri shot back, clutching the lavender pendant hanging from the necklace around her neck. "A lot of people pre-judge me and call me conceited just because I'm light-skinned, and they don't even know me. They assume that I think I'm *all that* just because of my light skin color. Even my own family puts me down because I'm the lightest one. Sometimes my own cousins would say that I think I'm better than them just 'cause I got good hair and that I couldn't relate to what they go through with their hair. My sister, who is browner than me, would claim that my mom would treat me better just because I'm lighter than her. I used to be depressed because I wanted nothing more than to fit in with my family; with my blood. So I started to study the history of beautiful, strong black women to get more in touch with my roots. Soon, I let the perm grow out of my hair and went natural. I learned that it's not natural or healthy for us black women to be putting chemicals in our hair and weaves in our hair and—"

"So whatchu tryna say, huh?!" Karisma yelled, standing up out of her seat and slamming her fists into the desk. "You tryna say me and my girl Mahogany ain't natural 'cause we got weaves? Huh? You tryna say we fake? Yo, I'll come up there and—"

"My sista! I come in love, light, and peace," Zuri jumped back in. "I would never put down one of my fellow sistas. I'm just tryna lift you up. Just like I did to my best friend, Imani. I taught her that one reason why a lot of black girls' hair doesn't grow the way we want it to is because of poor nutrition and relaxer damage. All the chemicals and perms we put in our hair is burning our scalp. Constant combing and pulling it back too tight thins the edges. So now, Imani wears her hair natural, like me. Like we all should."

"Myself, personally, I like girls with long hair," Milk announced, beaming in his chair.

"Mee too," Myles agreed, bumping fists with Milk.

"My hair is long," Zuri said, running her hand through her natural curls.

"When I say long, I mean straight down to your shoulders long. Not up like yours," Myles explained.

"Most black girls' hair grows upwards towards the sun, like plants and flowers," Zuri declared. "It's my crown. That's how my hair naturally grows, so why change that?"

"But everyone can't grow their hair naturally to look like yours," Mahogany challenged.

"Yeah, and weaves look good and gives girls like me confidence," Karisma argued. "If you can't get your hair to naturally grow to your shoulders, then ain't nothing wrong with a weave."

"Everything is wrong with that, sista," Zuri objected. "When we get weaves, we're trying not to look like the way the Universe made us."

"I did a research paper last year on black women's hair, and did you know that black women alone spend 500 million a year in hair care products?" Imani revealed. "Selling hair and hair care products is a 500-million-dollar business."

"Wow, I'm in the wrong profession," Ms. Camara admitted, laughing to herself. "I need to own my own beauty supply store."

"You know what?" Big Snacks chimed in. "For all you young, beautiful ladies in here that was teased or made fun of because you are light- or dark-skinned or short or fat, I just want y'all to know that I don't discriminate. I love all y'all. So if you feeling depressed or unloved, come on and give Big Snacks a hug! Come on, all of y'all." Big Snacks stood up out of his seat, arms spread like an eagle, waiting for a hug from one of the young ladies.

"Boy, sit ya butt down!" Ms. Camara demanded with a wink and a smile. Then she added, "Well, we have ten minutes left before dismissal. We didn't discuss anything that I had planned for you on my agenda, but we had an excellent and insightful discussion, so that's okay. I'm going to dismiss you guys a little early, but before you go, I want to leave you guys with the first of our daily affirmations in this program."

"What's an affirmation?" Imani asked.

"Affirmations are short, powerful statements that can be life changing," Ms. Camara explained. "When you hear them over and over again, eventually they will become the thoughts, your thoughts, that create your reality. Unfortunately, for many of us who live in low-poverty areas, we are surrounded by so much negativity. Negative words, negative actions, negative thoughts; eventually the negativity becomes our reality. I'm hoping our daily affirmations can undo some of the negativity in our lives." Ms. Camara walked to the middle of the band room, glanced at the index card she was holding, looked around the room, and addressed the students. "Today's affirmation is: *I have people who care about me and will help me if needed.* Okay, now you guys say it out loud, together." As the class repeated the affirmation aloud, Ms. Camara noticed that one of the girls wasn't participating. "Excuse me, young lady with the hoody on. What is your name?"

"Noni," she mumbled.

"Noni Wyatt?" Ms. Camara repeated, looking down at the attendance sheet attached to the clipboard. Noni responded by folding her arms, forming a nest, and laying her head in it.

"Noni, please remove your hoody." Noni sucked her teeth, rolled her eyes, and removed the hoody from her head.

"I noticed that you weren't repeating the affirmation with the rest of the class. Is there a reason why?"

"I ain't feel like it!" Noni snapped.

"Well, I'm pretty sure you have someone in your life that cares about you and will help you if you need it," Ms. Camara assured, calm in her voice.

"I'm pretty sure you're wrong," Noni snapped off again. "Nobody cares about me!"

"Come on, girl," Big Snacks spoke up. "I'm sure ya moms or someone cares about—"

"Mind ya business, fat boy! Ain't nobody talkin' to you!" The class erupted with laugher, pointing at Big Snacks.

"Alright class, calm down!" Ms. Camara announced, banging a yard stick on the desk to get the students' attention. "Listen, we are going to end on a positive note. What I'm about to say is for Noni and all of you. I care about each and every single one of you. If any of you ever need me, I will definitely help you! And on that note, everyone have a good night! I will see you all in school tomorrow and back here tomorrow afternoon."

"Hurry up, Mahogany," Karisma urged in a whisper. "I'm gonna catch Imani in front of the school and drag that chick up and down the block for calling me black. Come on!" As students were filing out, Ms. Camara called out to Mahogany, Karisma, and Noni, "Wait behind with me, I need to talk to you ladies."

"Can't," Noni muttered as she brushed by Ms. Camara. "Got things to do." Ms. Camara stood idly by as Noni stepped into the hallway and disappeared around the corner.

"What did *we* do?!" Karisma shouted, arms spread like a soaring bird, the palms of her hands facing the ceiling.

"I didn't say you did anything, Karisma. I just need to talk to you two." Karisma glared at the back of Imani's and Zuri's heads as they exited the room, upset at the missed opportunity.

"I wonder what she wants to talk to us about?" Mahogany said. Karisma and Mahogany sat uncomfortably in their seats, waiting to find out what they did wrong.

Chapter 14

Can't get you off my mind, regrettin' what I did to you/
my soul's being punished and my heart's doin' a prison bid for you/

Mahogany and Karisma followed Ms. Camara into her office. "Have a seat. I want to show you ladies something." Ms. Camara removed a scrapbook from the bookshelf and placed it on her cluttered desk. "I was listening to you ladies earlier in the band room, and it's pretty obvious that y'all have a complex about having dark brown skin." Mahogany and Karisma shamefully bowed their heads as Ms. Camara continued. "I can definitely relate because when I was your age, I too was uncomfortable in my own dark brown skin. You know, kids are so cruel. They would make fun of me and call me all kinds of names—tar-baby, blacky. I would go home and cry almost every day. At night, I would pray to God to make me lighter in the morning. Then, one day my grandmother and I had a discussion, and she educated me on our history. Our real history. Showed me that we black girls come from greatness. I want to show you girls something." Ms. Camara opened the scrapbook, and the girls leaned in to get a better look. "My grandmother encouraged me to start a scrapbook and collect pictures and stories of beautiful brown-skinned women. As I stared at their pictures and read their stories, it comforted me and made me proud of my skin color."

"Who is that?" Mahogany asked, pointing at one of the pictures on the first page.

"That's Madam CJ Walker. The first female self-made millionaire."

"How did she become a millionaire?" Karisma asked.

"She was an entrepreneur and developed and marketed a line of beauty and hair products."

"Entrepreneur means to own your own business, right?" Mahogany asked.

"Yup. And she owned her own business during the early 1900s. Just fifty years after slavery ended. Not only were these difficult times for black people, but it was especially tough for black women. But she believed in herself when others didn't, at a time when women didn't have any rights in the eyes of many."

"No disrespect, but she's old. I mean really old," Karisma chuckled. "Do you have any black women in here who are a little younger?"

"A little younger, sure," Ms. Camara answered, flipping to the next page. "This is Mary McLeod Bethune. She was a teacher and opened up a high school, a hospital, and the Daytona Literacy and Industrial Training School for black girls. Eventually she became the president of the National Association of Colored Women and then the National Council of Negro Women and fought for our civil rights." Ms. Camara flipped to the next page. "And this is Shirley Chisholm, the first African American congresswoman. She was also the first African American woman to run for president."

"Wow, and all this time I thought Hillary Clinton was the first woman to run for president," Mahogany said.

"Okay, let me rephrase what I said," Karisma began, chuckling. "Do you have any black women in here that is still alive?" Ms. Camara flipped a few more pages. "Who's that?" Karisma asked.

"Lauryn Hill!" Ms. Camara answered.

"Who?"

"You don't know Lauryn Hill?"

"No, never heard of her," Karisma confessed, shaking her head.

"Me neither," Mahogany chimed in.

"I can't believe y'all never heard of Lauryn Hill!" Ms. Camara exclaimed. "She sings, she raps, and in my opinion, she is the greatest female rapper, ever." The girls stared blankly at Ms. Camara. She laughed and flipped through her scrapbook, stopping on certain pages and pointing out specific pictures. "This is Charnele Brown, who played Kim Reese on my favorite show, *A Different World*. And this is

Regina King, and on the next page is Kelly Rowland from the group Destiny's Child—"

"Hey, ain't that Beyoncé's old group?" Karisma asked.

"Yes, it is."

"See, I know a little something about old-school groups," Karisma stated proudly. Ms. Camara removed two more scrapbooks from the bookshelf. "I want you guys to start your own scrapbooks," Ms. Camara said, handing the two empty scrapbooks to each one of the girls. "Similar to mine, make a collection of beautiful, strong, brown-skinned women with powerful stories. And hopefully your scrapbooks will be therapeutic and help you fully embrace your skin color, as it did for me."

"I don't even know where to begin to look for pictures or who to look for," Mahogany confessed.

"You can look on the internet and through magazines," Ms. Camara answered, removing an *Essence* magazine from the shelf. "You can start with this picture of Lupita Nyong'o, who played in *12 Years a Slave*. Do you see how beautiful her brown skin is?"

"It *is* beautiful," Mahogany agreed. "Looks like her skin is glowing."

"Ohhh, Tika Sumpter is in here. That's my picture," Karisma claimed before grabbing a pair of scissors and cutting out the picture. Over the next ten minutes, Mahogany and Karisma selected and cut out pictures for their scrapbooks.

"Okay, ladies," Ms. Camara said as Mahogany and Karisma were gathering loose paper scraps and tossing them into the garbage bin. "It's time to go. I will see you ladies tomorrow. Just promise me you guys will continue to add pictures to your scrapbook."

"I will," Karisma promised.

"I promise," Mahogany assured. The girls gathered their backpacks and scrapbooks and exited the school building.

On her way home, Mahogany texted her mom, asking if it would be all right to visit Tafari in the hospital. Mom responded that it would be okay, so Mahogany dropped off her backpack and scrapbook at home, then took the bus to Jacobi Hospital.

On the long bus ride to the hospital, Mahogany envisioned Tafari wrapped up like an Egyptian mummy, lying in agony on his bed and barely able to speak. But to her relief, when she crept into Tafari's hospital room, he was sitting up in his bed with thick headphones covering his ears. Quickly Tafari removed the headphones when he spotted Mahogany.

Mahogany thought she saw a slight twinkle in Tafari's eyes, but it went dim before she was sure. She thought she saw a smirk, but then again it could have been a frown. It looked as if Tafari wanted to smile, frown, laugh, and cry all at the same time. After what felt like a minute-long staring contest, Mahogany broke the silence. "I'm so happy that you're okay," Mahogany said, eyeing the white bandage covering Tafari's shoulder.

"I'm happy that you came to visit me, because I didn't think you cared anymore," Tafari confessed.

"Whatchu mean?"

"After what happened the last time we saw each other, I didn't think you—"

"As upset as I was witchu the last time we saw each other, and as much as I wanted you to suffer for what you did to me, I didn't want to see you get shot and possibly die," Mahogany admitted. "I might have said to myself I wanted you to die when I was walking away from the pizza shop and you were sitting with Malikah, but I didn't mean it literally."

"Thanks, I guess." Tafari chuckled nervously.

"Hey, where's ya mom?"

"She went out to get us something to eat. She should be back soon." Mahogany nodded and Tafari continued, "But on another note, I'm feelin' ya hair. It looks really good on you."

"Thank you." Mahogany blushed, taking a seat in the chair beside the bed. "Well, how are you feeling?"

"I still have some pain in my shoulder. Luckily this IV is numbing most of the pain because it could be a lot worse. Other than that, I'm good. I mean, I'm alive, right?"

"Yeah, thank God for that. But let me ask you…was it…um," Mahogany paused and scanned the room, making sure they were alone. "Was it Donovan that shot you?"

"Donovan?!"

"Yeah, you remember him. The guy that was with Dready on the train. I heard you took his girlfriend's chain in school and—"

"How you know 'bout that?!" Tafari wondered, quizzical expression on his face.

"I was there when him and his friends were talking about it."

"Why were you hanging around Donovan and his friends?"

"I was at a hooky party."

"A hooky party?!"

"Yeah, my boyfriend was having a hooky party and—"

"Boyfriend! Hold up, hold up. You gotta boyfriend?"

"Yes! Why do you sound so shocked that I have a boyfriend?"

"I'm not shocked. It's just that—"

"It's just that, what? I'm too ugly to get another boyfriend?"

"Of course not."

"You think you the only guy that can like me?"

"No, it's just that I can't picture you with anybody else besides me."

"You should have thought about that before you played me for Malikah."

"Well, back to what you said earlier," Tafari said, changing the subject. "Why did you think it was Donovan that shot me?"

"Because." Mahogany paused to scan the area again. "When Donovan shot Timothy, he was actually looking for you."

"It was Donovan that shot Timothy!?"

"Yeah."

"You sure about that?"

"Yeah. My boyfriend was with him when it happened. Donovan was actually looking for you because you embarrassed him. He saw two guys on the corner and he thought one of them was you. But it turns out that the person he thought was you, was Timothy."

"So, basically, I'm the reason why Timothy is dead," Tafari declared, sealing his eyelids shut as if trying to squeeze in the tears.

"It's not your fault."

"It is my fault. That bullet had my name on it. If it wasn't for something I did, Timothy would still be alive." Tafari bowed and shook his head slowly.

"You can't blame yaself for Donovan escalating the situation," Mahogany reasoned. "If he wanted to pay you back, all he had to do was rob you or beat you up or something. He didn't have to try to kill you."

"You're right, he didn't have to try to kill me, but he's a street dude. When you got beef with street dudes, street stuff happens."

"So, if Donovan didn't shoot you, who did?"

"Don't worry about it."

"How could I not worry about you? You could have been killed."

"I'm not saying don't worry about me. I'm just saying, don't worry about my situation. I don't want to involve you."

"Why not?"

"Just…just drop it. By the way, who told you that I got shot?"

"Mr. Sekou."

"I didn't know you had Mr. Sekou for English."

"I don't. But I had to attend his after-school program this afternoon, and he told the class that he had to leave early because he was going to attend Timothy's vigil at his apartment and then he was going to visit you, here at the hospital."

"You had to attend the S.I.C.K program? Why?"

"For fighting."

"You, fighting? Wow! I guess your hair ain't the only thing that changed about you."

"Actually, I was trying to break up a fight, but Mr. Sullivan assumed I was involved, and I got suspended."

"Was there a guy named Angel in the after-school program today?"

"No, he wasn't there. Why? You know him?"

"Yeah, something like that."

"He's one of my boyfriend's friends."

"Really? What's ya boyfriend's name?"

"Makai."

"I don't know him. But it's crazy that your boyfriend is friends with two dudes I got beef with. Why you going out with a street dude? It's not like you to be messin' with thugs."

"Excuse me! I went out with you, didn't I?"

"Yeah, but when you found out I had a gun, you was about to break up with me."

"I thought about breaking up with you, but then I was ready to give you a second chance until you—" Mahogany paused to dab the corners of her eyes with her fingertips. "I get so angry at you when I think back to what you did to me."

"What did I do to make you so angry?"

"Is that a serious question?" Mahogany asked rhetorically. "Where do I begin? First, you weren't man enough to tell me that you didn't want to be with me anymore. If it wasn't for Vaughn, I would have never found out. Then in the pizza shop, you didn't stand up for me when your new girlfriend embarrassed me in front of everybody."

"Oh…um…look, Mahogany, I'm…I'm sorry," Tafari stammered.

"Oh, now you sorry."

"You make it seem like I'm the one that made that joke about you."

"You might as well have. You just stood there and did nothing. We've known each other since we were like five years old. I thought we were friends. I thought we were close. I thought we were…" The last few words got caught in the lump that formed in Mahogany's throat. Tears streamed from her eyes and moistened her cheeks.

It looked as if Tafari wanted to say something, but he couldn't find the words. Instead he placed his hand on Mahogany's shoulder to comfort her.

"What happened to us, Tafari?" Mahogany whined. "We used to go to Bible study together. We used to talk on the phone all the time. And, we had just become boyfriend and girlfriend—"

"I think that's it right there," Tafari interrupted.

"What's it?"

"The part about us becoming boyfriend and girlfriend. That was the start of the end right there."

"But I don't understand."

"I don't expect you to understand. It's a man thing."

"You ain't a man!"

"You know what I mean," Tafari snapped.

"Well, help me understand, because you're not making any sense to me right now." Mahogany watched as Tafari's eyes searched the floor, as if the answer were written between the tiled lines. But Mahogany knew that Tafari knew better. The answers lay between the lines of his brain.

Tafari took a deep breath and exhaled. "That night on the train changed my life. It changed who I was. Once I became your boyfriend, I was supposed to protect you, know what I'm sayin'? Like any man is supposed to. And that night when Dready and Donovan entered our car and did what they did, making me look like a lame, I couldn't face you anymore. That night on the train, I lost my pride, dignity, self-esteem—everything. I knew in order to survive on them streets, I had to recreate myself. So that's what I did. I changed my whole image. And when I did that, I escaped the world my mom created for me and entered a new world. The world on the streets. And once you're in that world, like the commercial says, image is everything. You do whatever you gotta do to protect that image. So everything associated with my old world, I had to cut off. Vaughn was a lame and an image killer, so I had to cut him off. I also had to cut off—

"Me!" Mahogany said.

"What?"

"You had to cut me off too, didn't you?"

"Nah, I didn't completely cut you off. I mean, like I said, image or your reputation is all you got when you on the streets. I changed the way I dressed, spoke, who I hung out with, and who I liked."

"Who you liked? So you mean to tell me you just stopped liking me, just like that?"

"I never stopped liking you. It's just that, I thought you didn't fit in to that new world I was a part of."

"So being with Malikah helped your image?"

"Heck yeah. Malikah is the goddess of the projects. All the thugs wanted her. But she wanted to be with me. How could I turn her down? I felt like I was the *man* when I was with her. All eyes were on us, wherever we went."

"You like the attention, but do you really *like* her?"

"I definitely like the way she looks," Tafari chuckled. "I mean, she's light-skinned, she got long hair and a bangin' body. She got it all. She's beautiful. But I have to admit, sometimes she's not very pretty on the inside. Her attitude and her personality can be ugly at times."

"She don't care about you or the person you really are on the inside. If she did, she wouldn't treat you the way she does. I be seeing her."

"Seeing her do what?"

"I have seen her in the staircase and in the halls walking with different dudes."

"She told me she has a lot of male friends."

"Do you be smiling and cheesin' and whispering to your friends just inches from their faces? Do you embrace your friends every time you see them? Do your friends buy you lunch all the time?"

"I didn't know she was doing all that," Tafari grunted, gnawing on his bottom lip. "But it doesn't surprise me."

"What's funny is, you thought going out with her would help your rep, but the things she's doing to you behind your back is actually hurting your rep. All those people looking at you and Malikah when you were together are probably laughing at you behind your back." Tafari looked dumbfounded. Then he looked as if he were searching for the words but couldn't find any that would make for a sensible response.

"I would have never done anything like that to you," Mahogany admitted. "You didn't have to change your image and recreate yourself, because I loved you for who you were on the inside. Now I don't know who you are anymore."

"Dang, I guess I messed up, huh?"

"Messed up how?"

"I...um..." Tafari paused and reached for the black-and-white composition notebook that was underneath a thesaurus on the stand beside his bed. "I can rap it to you better than I can say it to you."

"Whatchu mean?"

"I wrote a song for you."

"For me? Why?"

"Having a near-death experience has a way of making a person reflect on his life. Well, not my whole life, but the last couple months. I just been thinking about some of the choices I made and some of the regrets I have. One of my biggest regrets is you."

"What about me?" Tafari flipped the pages until he found the page he was looking for.

"The rhyme is kinda long, so I'll just pick it up in the middle. Tafari cleared his throat, "Check it," and rhymed straight from the page...

You're wrapped in a beautiful sheet of golden-brown ebony skin/

a mix of mocha and macchiato, a Starbucks-style heavenly blend/

But in a world where color matters, it's hard to maintain control/

forgettin' hymns, committin' sins, just to ease the pain in ya soul/

You're a queen, a daughter, a sister, an artist, a leader/

an angel, a goddess, a provider, a healer, a teacher/

Ya kinky hair and full lips may seem like an odd privilege/

But when you look in the mirror you're seeing the reflection of God's image/

Can't get you off my mind, I'm regrettin' what I did to you/

my soul's being punished and my heart's doin' a prison bid for you/

You loved me before my name was hood famous, before the mix tape/

Before my crew of thugs, before I popped my first gun in the staircase/

They devalued you, embarrassed you, and I didn't protect you/

I stood by as a joke killed your soul but now I wanna help resurrect you/

Reconnect wit' you, get back together, pick up where we left off/

Rebuild and heal together and massage the stress off/

Tafari lowered his rhyme book from his eyes and glanced into Mahogany's. She felt water in them. Mahogany noticed water in his too. Tafari cleared his throat again. "Remember when you asked me on the train, why can't I write a rhyme about love?"

A lump the size of a jawbreaker grew in Mahogany's throat. She swallowed before stammering, "Um...yeah...I remember."

"I still need to write another verse. I'mma call this song, 'Darkskin and Redbones.' So whatchu think?"

"Why you gotta call it 'Darkskin and Redbones'?"

"Because that's how it all started. Malikah cracking a joke about your beautiful brown skin. Then a fight breaks out all because a light-skinned girl insulted a dark-skinned girl. I wrote this song because I want you to know how beautiful you are and how ignorant Malikah was."

Mahogany didn't respond; she just wiped more tears. The door creaked open, and Tafari's mom entered, holding a box of pizza.

"Hey, Mahogany!" Tafari's mom cheered. "Long time no see. How have you been, sweetie?"

"I'm okay, Ms. King," Mahogany said, drying the corners of her eyes as she rose up out of her seat.

"Are you sure, sweetie?" Ms. King wondered, embracing Mahogany as if she were her own daughter. "You don't look okay."

"I'm fine, Ms. King. It's just that..." Mahogany paused and took a backward glance at Tafari. "I gotta go."

Mahogany peeled herself away from Ms. King's embrace and headed for the door.

"Don't leave. Stay and have pizza with us. There's plenty."

"Thanks, but I can't."

"Why not?"

"I gotta get home before it gets too dark. You know how my mom is."

"Okay, sweetie. Send ya mom my blessings."

"I will."

"And tell her I said to call me."

"Okay, I will. Bye." Mahogany ducked out of the hospital room and headed toward the bus stop. As Mahogany settled into a seat on the bus, she sealed her eyelids shut and sighed as she reflected on her long day. Visions of napping on her soft bed comforted her during the long bus ride.

Chapter 15

They devalued you, embarrassed you, and I didn't protect you/ I stood by as a joke killed your soul but now I wanna help resurrect you/

"Ouuuwwww!" Mahogany yelped as a flaming sting across the back of her thighs snatched her out of sleep's gentle caress. Mom's blurry face hovered just above Mahogany's. Her eyes were slit with anger and her lips were drawn in above her chin. "Is this yours!" Mom barked, flashing a condom still in its wrapper across Mahogany's blurred vision. "And don't you dare lie to me!" Mom was violently shaking a worn leather belt in the air.

Mahogany's brain was short-circuiting. She couldn't form a proper response. It was kind of hard to concentrate on forming sentences when that leather belt was swaying in front of her eyes like a dancing cobra. "Um..."

"*Um*'s not a answer!" Mom's arm sliced through the air, and the worn leather belt smacked against the back of Mahogany's legs again.

"Mommy no! Please, Mommy!" Mahogany squealed, curled up on the bed. Melani hovered in the back, eyes bubbling with curious excitement. The expression on Melani's face tipped Mahogany off as to where Mom got the condom. Mahogany cursed in her mind when she realized she'd left it on the bathroom sink the other day.

"And, I'm hearing that you sneaked a boy in this house, in this room, without my permission? Is this true!?" Mahogany nodded and curled into a tight ball, anticipating a third lash. Mom dropped the belt at her feet and clenched her fists and eyes. She inhaled, deeply, threw her hands up, and cursed as she stormed out of the room.

"Jehovah, Lord, give me strength!" Mahogany heard her mom cry out. "Give me the strength to not kill this girl, Jehovah! Help me, Jehovah! Help me!" The bedroom door was open, so Mahogany could see in her mother's room and watched her kneel down and genuflect beside her bed. Mahogany looked around and didn't see any signs of Melani. Melani! The thought of Melani filled her gut with rage and warmed Mahogany's skin from the inside out. Before Mahogany knew it, she was out of the bed, zombie-walking toward the kitchen.

Melani had just removed a plate of baked chicken and yellow rice from the microwave and placed it on the table. Feeling Mahogany's presence, she quickly turned to face her. The look on Mahogany's face must have been psychotic because horror flashed across Melani's face.

"You just couldn't help yaself, could you?" Mahogany grunted.

"What are you talking about?"

"You snitched on me. Didn't you?"

"I...um...I..." Melani stammered. Mahogany's teeth gnawed on her bottom lip as she moved closer. Melani backed up. Her eyes were darting around, looking for an exit. Mahogany reached for the countertop and grabbed a butter knife.

The knife ascended over Mahogany's head and swooped down toward Melani's face. Melani reached up and caught Mahogany's right wrist. The butter knife was suspended in mid-air, just inches away from Melani's face. "MAAAAAA!" Melani screamed.

Mahogany's left hand jumped up and grabbed a handful of Melani's thick hair. She yanked it down until Melani's back hit the tiles. Mahogany tumbled on top of her. "You ain't my sister!" Mahogany yelled in Melani's face. "You a snitch! I hate you!" The two combatants rolled around with the knife still inches from Melani's left eye.

"Stop it! Stop it!" Mom yelled, racing down the hall.

Mom rushed toward them and grabbed Mahogany by the waist, pulling her off of Melani. Anger flowed down Mahogany's arm like adrenaline. It stiffened up like a board and swung back, striking Mom across the chest. She tumbled back, knocking Melani's plate off of the kitchen table. Rice rained down like confetti, scattering across the floor and Mom's face as she lay half under the table. Melani managed to stumble to her feet and trip across the tiles to the other side of the table. Following closely behind Melani like a heat-seeking missile, Mahogany cornered Melani between the kitchen table and the wall and moved in on her like a masked killer from a second-rate eighties horror movies.

Melani screamed to the top of her lungs and wildly swung her arms and kicked her feet. Mahogany lunged at her, brittle side of the butter knife first. The knife got caught up in Melani's swinging arms like a blender and spun out, flying across the air and tumbling into a corner. Her arms continued to swing as if she were turning double Dutch. Mahogany's fists danced outside of her arms, hesitating and waiting before jumping through the first opening she saw and jabbing her in the mouth. She punched her sister as if her fist were shoving Melani's snitching words back down her throat. While Melani clutched her mouth, Mahogany rushed at her and grabbed another handful of her hair. She reeled Melani's head into her body, threw her arm around her neck, and squeezed like a vise. With Melani in the headlock, Mahogany slid her hips under Melani's torso and flipped her over, slamming her onto the floor. The force of the slam caused Mahogany to tumble on top of her. As Mahogany raked her fingernails across the side of Melani's face, Melani reached around and grabbed a handful of Mahogany's hair and yanked her head back. Mahogany returned the favor. Both girls were forced to look up at the ceiling, screaming and howling at one another to let go.

Mom rushed over and dragged Mahogany off of Melani. When Mahogany climbed to her feet, Mom shoved her into the hall. Still enraged, Mahogany reached over her mother, trying to get at Melani. A sharp elbow sliced across Mom's high cheekbone as she leapt. Mom stumbled away, holding her right eye, but Mahogany didn't notice. Mahogany ran back into the kitchen and perfectly executed a flying tackle like she was a W.W.E. wrestler. She pinned down Melani on the kitchen floor, longer than a three-count. Through her peripheral vision, Mahogany saw Mom pick up the phone and then frantically scream the address in the receiver. She slammed the phone down and dove on Mahogany's back as if she were Melani's tag-team partner.

"Get off her! Get off her!" Mom screamed. She wrapped her arm around Mahogany's neck and dragged her across the kitchen. Mahogany wrestled herself free from the chokehold and stumbled to her feet.

"Get outta my house, now!" Mom yelled in her face.

"You can't be serious?!"

"Either leave now or leave in handcuffs!"

"You called the cops on me?"

"Yes, I want you outta here! Now!" Mahogany was numb. She didn't *want* to believe Mom's words, but it was something about the way she said it. Something about the way that frown screwed into her mom's face and the way her throaty words drilled deep within Mahogany, nailing into her core, that made Mahogany know that Mom was dead serious.

Mahogany was as discombobulated as she looked: her hair was frizzy and out of place, her long Minnie Mouse nightgown was twisted and bunched up, leaving her tan panties showing for all to see.

Is this really happening? Mahogany thought to herself. The sound of police sirens on the other side of the window sent chill bumps ripping up Mahogany's spine and answered the questions circulating in her mind. *Oh my God, this is real.* Mahogany stormed into her bedroom and quickly pulled on the first pair of blue jeans she grabbed from her closet. She stepped into her sneakers without bothering to put on socks and grabbed her cell phone and her jacket. After opening the front door, Mahogany glanced back to get one last look at her mother. Mom was stroking Melani's hair, who was lying on her shoulder, weeping. Anger pooled back into her gut. But that time, Mom was the cause of it. "You love Melani more than you love me!" Mahogany spat. "I'm your daughter too! But you always taking her side! And I know why! It's because I'm darker than her and you love her more!" Mahogany cut her eyes at both of them and slammed the door.

Mahogany leaned back against the wall beside the apartment door and slid down into a seat on the floor. She hugged her knees to her chest, allowing her head to rest on her hard kneecaps. *There is no way Mom is going to let her youngest daughter sit out here for too long,* Mahogany thought to herself. *She just tryna teach me a lesson.* The rage that was bubbling deep within the well of her feelings had boiled over into a soupy, thick pool of sorrow. Her chest began heaving and her shoulders tensed up. Tears were flowing. Clear snot dribbled from her flared nostrils. The pool of sorrow had spilled from the inside and was now all over her face.

Mahogany's heart was pounding when she snapped her head up and scanned the unfamiliar surroundings. She couldn't figure out why she wasn't in bed. Once Mahogany shook the sleepy fog from her head, she remembered that she was *put out*. Mahogany checked the time on her cell phone and realized she had been in the hallway for an hour. The cops hadn't shown up yet. Either Mom didn't really call them or the cops were late as usual when called to the projects. Either way, Mahogany was still in the hallway. And she knew now, at that moment, Mom wasn't going to let her back in. The tears and snot dried up. The pool of sorrow had hardened into a pit of cold reality in her gut.

Makes me wanna holla, rang out in her head. Mahogany closed her eyes and used her mind's eye to go back inside the apartment, two hours ago, and see her mom's face twisted in anger. The last and only time she ever saw her mom so angry was when she called the cops on her dad before ordering him to leave the apartment.

She wondered if her dad had sat beside the door, like she was doing? And did he wait, hoping Mom would open the door? And when she didn't, did cold reality lift him off the floor and push him toward the path that led to her grandmother's building?

Mahogany thought back to the conversation she had with Karisma, about not seeing her dad in years and the need to go see him. *There's no better time than now*, Mahogany thought.

Similar to the way she imagined her dad had left, Mahogany rose up from her seat in the hallway, stepped out of her building, and allowed cold reality to guide her as she traced her dad's envisioned footsteps to Grandma's building. It was near dusk, and it dawned on her that Dad didn't have any footprints leading back home. Mahogany hadn't figured out that part yet. The part about finding her way back home. A part of her was hopeful that in the morning, Mom would have a change of heart and show her the way. The rest of her was looking forward to the freedom.

CPSIA information can be obtained
at www.ICGtesting.com
Printed in the USA
LVOW08s1619120418
573254LV00001B/67/P